D1312961

BROTHERLY LOVE

Lorna Peel

Author's Note

There was a huge increase in Ireland's population in the early nineteenth century. By 1831, it was 7,767,401, and this led to great competition amongst tenant farmers for available land. Because of this, landlords could charge high rents and evict tenants, as they knew many others were crying out for land.

The Ribbon Society was a secret society whose objective was to control rent rises and prevent landlords from evicting their tenants, many of whom lived in miserable conditions in single-roomed mud cabins on small plots of land. Their members, called Ribbonmen, attacked landlords, maimed their cattle, and damaged their property. Ribbonmen also destroyed the homes and crops of farmers renting the land of evicted tenants. They were most active between 1835 and 1855.

Faction fights were mass brawls at Irish fairs, markets, funerals, race meetings, and patterns (parish patron saints days) between hundreds, sometimes thousands, of people – usually families or parishes or estate tenants – whose weapons were usually sticks and stones. The fights often resulted in the deaths of one or more of the participants, and always resulted in maiming and injury. The tradition descended from one generation to the next as did the leadership of each faction.

Reasons for fighting ranged from a desire to display a family's strength, conflicts over non-payment of dowries, fights over succession to land, and long-standing grudges often going back several generations. In many cases, the reasons behind some grudges were so trivial that it was not unusual for members of hostile factions to live and work peacefully together except for the days when the factions gathered together to fight.

The sticks used in faction fights were of holly, oak, whitethorn, and blackthorn. The blackthorn stick was popular because it was thought that a cut or a wound from a blackthorn would heal more quickly than those from a whitethorn. Sticks were also weighted at one end to cause maximum injury.

The police's response to faction fights was to observe rather than to intervene unless there were threats to the upper classes, otherwise the constabulary only made arrests when the fighting had run its course. By 1839, it was reported that faction fighting had all but come to an end but in the decades following, old scores often flared up and faction fighting continued right up to the last recorded fight at Cappawhite, County Tipperary in 1887.

This book is written in British English. Spellings and grammatical conventions are conversant with the UK and Ireland.

Brotherly Love

Chapter One

Doon Parish, Ireland, 1835

Caitriona had attended wakes which had begun well before the person to be waked had drawn their last breath. This would be another. She sighed and looked behind her as the cottage door opened and an elderly couple peered inside before quickly retreating. She turned back to the bed, fervent murmuring barely audible from those gathered around it. Father Liam Warner, his prayers interrupted by a shout of laughter from outside, frowned to himself and ran his fingers around the inside of his collar but carried on. Another louder shout of laughter followed and Mary, Caitriona's sister-in-law, glared across the kitchen at the small window.

"Have they no respect at all?" she snapped.

"Ah, now, Mary, hush." Her husband, Thady, patted her hand. "Leave them be, it's only a bit of high spirits."

"High spirits while your mother is dying," she raged.

5

Father Warner glared at her and Mary quickly bent her head again.

Caitriona stood and quietly lifted her chair back from the bed. Dropping her rosary beads into the pocket of her black cotton dress, she opened the cottage door and left the stifling heat of the kitchen.

Closing the door, she glanced around her. At least thirty people had congregated in front of the thatched cottage, seated on upturned tin buckets, sitting on the remains of the rick of turf, or just leaning against the whitewashed wall. When she was noticed, a few polite men stood up, pulling clay pipes from their mouths and removing their hats. One of them – Tommy Gilleen – edged forward, producing a fiddle from the depths of his blue coarse woollen coat.

"Has she gone, ma'am?"

"She has not gone," Caitriona replied. "But it won't be long. Father Warner has just anointed her. Please stop them making so much noise, Tommy, you'll all have time for that later when she has."

Tommy shrank back from her, quickly hiding the fiddle under his coat. "I'm sorry, ma'am, we didn't mean to be disrespectful."

Caitriona sighed. "No, well—" She stopped, catching sight of Michael Warner – the priest's brother – on the mountain path, unbuttoning his coat of fine black wool, and halting with his hands on his hips to catch his breath after the steep climb. "It shouldn't be long now," she added, turning back to Tommy. "But please be quiet. Let Bridget go in peace. God knows she's seen little enough of it during her life."

Tommy and many of the other men moved uncomfortably and peered down at the stout blackthorn sticks at their sides. Caitriona looked down at their sticks, let them see that she was looking at their sticks, then opened the door and went back inside.

Michael Warner turned off the mountain path just as Caitriona Brady closed the door. The large gathering outside the cottage appeared glum so he took off his hat.

"Has she gone?" he asked the man nearest to him.

"No." Danny Mullen chuckled. "The old girl's still to the good."

"Then why was Mrs Brady outside?" Michael frowned and saw Tommy Gilleen run his fingers over his stick. "What were you doing now?" he demanded.

"Nothing," Tommy replied angrily. "Just having a bit of fun, that's all. Waiting for the old girl to go."

"Fun?" Michael glared at him. "That old woman's been dying for months."

"Aragh, don't you start, we've just been told."

Tommy walked away and sat down on an upturned bucket but immediately jumped to his feet as they heard a long, high-pitched wail from inside the cottage. A few moments later the door opened and Caitriona Brady came outside, pulling a black fringed shawl around her shoulders. She pressed her lips together before sighing as everyone waited expectantly.

"Bridget Brady is dead," she announced and each person crossed themselves. "May she rest in peace." Mrs Brady walked out through the gathering who were now clamouring to get inside to pay their respects and get at the whiskey and tobacco. She stood on the path, stared out over the valley then down towards the village of Doon, inhaling and exhaling another long breath.

"Mrs Brady?" Hearing his voice, she spun around, and Michael nodded to her. "I'm sorry for your trouble."

"My trouble?" she repeated and smiled humourlessly, rolling her eyes to heaven. "Bridget Brady was trouble to me, if that's what you mean, Mr Warner."

He moved awkwardly from one foot to the other. "Well, I had heard the two of you didn't get on," he said diplomatically and she just smiled again and held her shawl tight to her throat as a strong gust of wind blew into their faces.

"I hated her and she hated me, Mr Warner. Everyone knows that and I'm telling you now, seeing as you're not long living in the parish. I wouldn't be wanting you to be getting the wrong end of the stick." She stamped her foot in frustration and he winced. That unfortunate expression certainly hadn't been the right one to use and he discreetly looked away. "If she'd had her way, I'd be the one lying in Doon graveyard, my face battered into nothingness – not John. My only crime was that I was his wife, and I was still alive to remind her every day that he wasn't. That was all."

"John Brady was a brave man and a good fighter, I heard," he said.

"John Brady was a fool," she said simply and Michael stared at her. She didn't sound very proud of him – a hero in many eyes. "A man's head can only take so much of a battering and John's took more than most. I told him to stop fighting – even his saintly mother told him to stop fighting – but he wouldn't."

"You must miss him," Michael added, wanting to see her reaction.

She remained impassive, which made him feel ill at ease. Surely a widow of only two years must still miss her husband?

He had seen John Brady's grave only the previous day, having gone to the graveyard with his brother. Brady had been beaten to death in a faction fight aged only thirty-seven, leaving behind a young widow but no children. Brady seemed to have been an awe-inspiring man – one of the local champions – and someone who was loved and hated equally by each side, judging by what Michael had heard about his death.

"No," she replied. "John loved his damned blackthorn stick and fighting more than he ever loved me. No wonder it was the death of him. And that woman—" She pointed back at the cottage." Every single day since he died I've had little jibes as to why I never fell pregnant. Well," she continued angrily, "all he wanted to do was fight. All he wanted to do in bed was sleep. No wonder there were no children, and I'm glad that there weren't, I had enough to put up with – with her."

Shrugging her shoulders, she smiled at his astonished expression. John Brady must have been mad to have only wanted to fight. When he had first heard of the Widow John Brady he had imagined her to be a withered old crone of eighty and not a beautiful young woman of twenty-five or so. Brady must have had all the brains knocked out of him to have not wanted his wife in bed. Dark brown curls were blowing around her face and neck and he was forced to make a pretence of rubbing his forehead in order to cover a flush which had spread across his cheeks.

"There you are." Both turned to see Liam walking towards them. He went to unbutton his black coat but another – even stronger – gust of wind forced him to abandon his plan. "If you don't hurry, you won't get anything to drink at all."

"I'm not thirsty, Father, thank you," Mrs Brady replied. "I hoped Mary looked after you?"

"Oh, yes, she did. Thank you."

"What about you, Mr Warner?" she asked, turning to him and he slowly lowered his hand, hoping he could trust his face.

"I'll look for a drink later, Mrs Brady, thank you," he replied quietly, his hand near his chin.

"Well, Bridget's with God now." Liam stood between them and they looked out over the valley. "She must have been a good age, from what I've heard."

"Seventy-three," Mrs Brady replied.

"And you?" Liam turned to her.

"I'm twenty-six, Father."

Liam smiled. "No, what I was going to say was, what are your plans?"

"My plans?" She stared at Liam and Michael grimaced. It was a bit early to start asking her that.

"Do you think it's safe for you to carry on living up here on this mountain now you're alone?"

"My mother-in-law and I have lived up here alone since my husband was killed," she replied stiffly.

Let her be for the time being, Michael told his brother silently. The mother-in-law wasn't even cold yet and Liam was starting this. From what he could make out, Mrs Brady was intent on enjoying herself and her new-found freedom. For the first time in her life, she was her own mistress and she was going to make the most of it.

"But your husband had many enemies, Mrs Brady," Liam persisted. "I'm only thinking of your safety."

"Father, if anything was going to happen to me, don't you think it would have happened long before now?"

Michael smiled to himself. Get out of that one, Liam.

"Your parents are from Dunmore Parish, aren't they? You could go home?"

"Home?" she exclaimed with clear revulsion. "No, Father, I will not go home. I am content here, thank you." With that, she turned on her heel and walked back to the cottage.

Michael immediately turned on his brother. "Leave her alone, Liam, for God's sake. Her mother-in-law hasn't even been buried yet."

"Her husband was loved and hated with intense ferocity, Michael. She could be set upon at any time. Do you know what that could spark off? This parish is in a bad enough state as it is for violence."

Michael frowned, he was beginning to see that. "Well, at least leave her be until the funeral is over, then talk to her; though, I doubt you'll get far."

"Yes, she is strong-willed." Liam glanced back at the cottage. "I just hope she sees sense."

Anyone entering the cottage and not seeing the deceased in the hag bed in the alcove near the fire would be forgiven if they assumed a wedding party was in full-flow, not a wake.

Caitriona stood at the door for a moment, watching as Tommy Gilleen seated himself on a three-legged stool near the fire and began to play his fiddle in direct competition to the women keening a lament at the bedside. A group soon gathered around him, tapping their feet and singing. What was it Tommy had said earlier about being disrespectful? She fought her way through the throng, went into the bedroom, and shut the door. She had just sat down on the bed when Mary came in without knocking.

"Happy now?" the older woman demanded, her eyes red and starting to look puffy.

"What?" Caitriona asked wearily. Surely Mary wasn't going to start a row with half the parish in the next room?

"You know damn-well what," Mary snapped. "You couldn't wait for her to die."

Caitriona remained silent for a moment, clearly disconcerting Mary somewhat, who had been expecting an outburst. Instead she spoke calmly.

"I nursed Bridget these last six months as you said you couldn't because of the children. Aren't children a blessing?"

"Well, you wouldn't know, would you?" Mary recovered quickly. "I mean, look at you – you always resented being matched with John – having to marry him and leave fancy Dunmore Parish for a life on a mountain. You never loved him, so it's no wonder he took to the fighting."

"You know full-well John fought ever since he was able to hold a stick." Caitriona smiled sweetly at her. "You're not jealous, are you, Mary? Of the fact that my husband didn't give up the fighting through lack of nerve?"

Mary's jaw dropped. "You bitch," she breathed. "You'll have to leave here, you know? You'll never manage living up here on a mountain on your own. You'll have to go home and I can only hope your parents can teach you some manners."

"I am not going home," Caitriona announced and Mary leaned back against the wall. "This is my home and my land now and I'm staying. Now, kindly get out of my bedroom." Her voice rose and the crowd in the next room fell silent.

Mary heaved herself away from the wall, flung open the door, and stomped across the kitchen to her husband. Caitriona got off the bed and walked to the door as Mary sat down with her back to her.

Caitriona looked around the larger of the two rooms in the cottage and everyone stared back at her, clearly wondering what she would have to say, and how she had managed to silence Mary Brady. Her eyes rested for a moment on Michael Warner, standing just inside the front door, before addressing them all.

"You're not slow to miss an argument, are you?" she asked with a weak smile. "Mary thinks that as I've no-one to look after anymore, I should leave here and go home to my parents in Dunmore. Well, I'm not going home," she stated firmly, widening her eyes to show that she really meant it. "I'm staying here, and anyone who has anything to say about it, then go ahead."

She waited for a moment or two but no-one made a move to speak. She nodded and continued;

"My husband is dead these two years. Now his mother is dead, too. I'm beholden to no-one now but myself. None of you can tell me what to do now, do you hear? My married name may be Brady but that doesn't mean I support one or other side in the fights around here. I don't support any side. I hate the fights, not just because they took away John, but because they are so meaningless. I was asked whether I felt safe here – whether I'd mind being alone here on the mountain. Well, I don't mind and I want you all to know that I am on no side, so no side can claim to fight on my behalf. I'm staying here, alone, and safe."

She smiled again, turned and went back into the bedroom, closing the door quietly behind her.

Chapter Two

When the door closed there was a deafening silence for about half a minute then a fevered whispering began. Michael and Liam stood motionless at the front door and glanced at each other. Liam, Michael noticed, was shaking his head.

"Damn the woman," he muttered.

"She's made her position clear, Liam," Michael protested. "She wants to stay here, so let her."

"And what if something happens to her?" his brother retorted. "Why can't she just go home to her parents?"

"Because this is her home now," Michael replied, moving aside to let a couple out.

"Lady Muck," the man was saying to his wife. "As if I'd fight for the likes of her, anyways."

Michael stared after them then caught Liam looking at him with a puzzled expression. He moved forward, a flush beginning to creep across his cheeks again and held out his glass for a fill of whiskey.

No-one came near Caitriona and she was glad. Well, quite glad. Not that she had expected Michael Warner to come into her bedroom. She flushed. She'd made her position quite clear to him earlier then again to everyone a few moments ago. She had looked at his face just before she turned away and he had appeared quite stunned. Maybe she had been too clear. Her flush deepened, but he didn't know that to get through to these people you had to be more than clear. Well, he knew now, that's for sure. She lay down on the bed, pulled her shawl around her, and closed her eyes. It was up to him now to make a move. She wasn't going to literally throw herself at him.

She smiled to herself. He was, by far, the most handsome man she had ever met. When she had seen him for the first time, someone had mistakenly told her he was the new priest. The disappointment she had felt had almost overwhelmed her until she had discovered the truth – the stocky forty-year-old with the receding hairline was the priest – and the tall, dark, and handsome twenty-eight-old was the brother.

Apart from his good looks, the fact that Michael had made a point of not allying himself with either faction had attracted her to him. He and his brother had lived just outside the village of Doon for over a year now and she had heard no reports of him having taken part in the fights, or having any interest in them. How long it would last she didn't know, but if he had managed to stay out of them this long...

"Caitriona can't speak to me like that." She couldn't help but overhear Mary, now right outside the bedroom door, giving out about her to poor Thady. "The hussy. Who does she think she is, at all?" There was a silence and Caitriona heard a thud and a groan. "Are you listening to me? She insulted you, too."

"Aragh, leave it, woman," Thady replied in a weary tone. "She'll soon get tired of living up here all on her own and go home to her parents."

"Don't you care?" Mary screeched over the keening which had begun again.

"No, but if you do so much, go and borrow Seanie Breen's stick and give her a couple of whacks with it if it'll make you feel better."

Caitriona couldn't help but smile at poor, hen-pecked Thady. He and John had been about as different in temperament as Michael and Liam Warner were in looks. Turning on her side, she closed her eyes.

Mary Brady glared at her husband and Michael turned away with a grin. Thady clearly didn't care what his sister-in-law said or did. But one thing Thady said did strike a chord with him and he frowned. Would Caitriona Brady get tired of living half-way up a mountain with only a cow, a calf, and some chickens for company? She was a very determined woman. Would she stay even if she did get tired of it – or afraid – just to prove herself?

He turned back and had a quick peek at the bedroom door, hoping she would have the sense to leave if things got too much for her. But if she didn't, he could always keep an eye on her. In secret, of course. He didn't know what she would do if she were to find out – and Liam – he glanced at his brother who was talking to Tommy Gilleen's wife. Liam saw

Mrs Brady as a bit of a nuisance, if not a bit dangerous.

He couldn't disregard what she had said about her surname but she was beautiful. He smiled down into his glass. She couldn't be a widow for the rest of her life. She needed some love. He couldn't be a bachelor for the rest of his life either. He'd keep a secret eye on her and take it from there.

Caitriona sighed with relief as Bridget Brady's coffin was lowered into the grave in Doon graveyard. You're really free now, she told herself, glancing at John's grave, right beside his mother's. All the Bradys together, I hope you'll both be very happy. You always were a mammy's boy, John, despite everything. She shook a few hands, ignoring Mary's glare, then moved away from the graves. It was time to go home. It was time to get on with her life.

"Are you sure you'll be all right, Mrs Brady?" Hearing a voice, she looked up into Father Warner's anxious face and smiled.

"I'll be fine, Father, thank you for asking," she replied as his brother walked over to them and shook her hand. His hand, although rough and hard, was also hot and sticky.

"Father Warner doesn't approve of my living alone on the mountain, Mr Warner," she informed him.

"He won't ever, I think." He smiled before growing serious. "If there's anything you need, Mrs Brady, just ask."

"Thank you." She took the opportunity of shaking his hand again before walking away.

"I'll give her two weeks up there," she heard the priest mutter to his brother as she closed the graveyard gate behind her.

Caitriona stood in the middle of the kitchen floor and looked around her. The cottage was hers. The rents from sub-letting ten out of the fifteen acres of land would be coming straight to her now, too. She spent the next half hour gathering all of Bridget's belongings together and piling them up at the door.

The next time she saw Thady or Mary she'd ask if they wanted them, otherwise she'd burn them.

Walking around the side of the cottage and shooing the six chickens out of her way, she gazed at her land bathed in late Spring sunshine and beyond it to her long and narrow turf bog plot. The first field fed Áine, the small black Kerry cow, and her calf. The second and third fields – full of potatoes and oats – fed her, and the oaten straw kept Áine going through winter. Any surplus eggs, butter, and milk was sold at the weekly market five miles away in Kilbarry.

On acquiring Tommy Gilleen as a tenant, following John's death, they had come to an agreement that Tommy would help her with both the oats and the turf in return for her help on his bog and a slight reduction in the rent. She had an income, she had food, and she had fuel. She nodded to herself, she'd be all right.

She went back inside for a bucket and retrieved some water from the stream which flowed past the cottage from a spring higher up on the mountain. Putting on her apron and rolling up her sleeves, she scrubbed the cottage from top to bottom – singing loudly as she worked – before going to bed tired but satisfied.

Bridget had never allowed her to sing to herself – loud or otherwise – she said that the noise made her head ache. In fact, the cottage had rarely been cleaned in the last few weeks of Bridget's life as the dust got on her chest. It had been evident at the wake, and Caitriona had seen Mary running her finger along the top of the dresser, the bitch.

Not wanting any reminders of her mother-in-law in the cottage and needing to pay Father Warner his dues for all his services, she decided to bring Bridget's belongings down to Thady and Mary the next day and kill two birds with one stone.

In the morning, she lifted a glass jar out of the bottom of the dresser and emptied the contents onto the kitchen table. Counting the coins, she blew out her cheeks in relief. She had just enough. She returned the empty jar to the dresser and dropped the coins into her pocket. Bundling Bridget's belongings into a sack, she set off down the mountain path to Doon village. She knocked at the Warners' roadside cottage but there was no reply. Walking to the L-shaped chapel, she found Father Warner at the altar and handed over the dues before continuing on.

Doon village grew up around a long-gone corn mill. It now consisted of a few shabby thatched cottages, one two-storey house-come-shop – now relegated to being the second building in the parish with a slate roof, thanks to the newly-built chapel – and a blacksmith's forge. There was fresh talk of a school being built, but there had been talk of a school being built when Caitriona had first come to the parish eight years ago and nothing had come of it.

Thady and Mary Brady and their three children lived half a mile the far side of the village, close to the ruins of the ancient church and graveyard of Doon. Thady, taking advantage of the good weather, was whitewashing the cottage. It was a messy job, he was covered in splashes from the water-based lime paint, and was grateful for the excuse to put the long horse hair brush down and take a break.

"I've brought you down your mother's things." She handed the sack to him, relieved she had seen him first and not Mary.

"It must be quiet up there now." Thady peered sadly at his mother's clothes.

"It is quiet," she admitted. "But I'm staying put."

Thady smiled. "You're a determined one."

She laughed and Mary came outside to see who was there. Mary scowled and turned to her husband.

"Have you done any work this morning?"

Thady held up the sack. "Caitriona's brought down Mammy's things."

Mary gave a short cough. "Trying to get rid of all trace of her, are you? I thought I could see smoke up on the mountain yesterday."

"Mary." Thady shouted at his wife and the two women jumped. Thady rarely raised his voice to his wife – rarely dared to. "It was kind of Caitriona to bring them down, it's a long old walk."

"Not for a lady of leisure who can take her time because she's got nothing else to do." Mary retorted and stomped back inside.

Caitriona curled her lip. Mary was impossible and she didn't know how Thady put up with someone who had an answer for everything.

"I know." He grinned knowingly at her. "I do get some peace and quiet sometimes."

"'Nothing else to do'." She gave him a grin. "You'd never think Mary didn't like me very much."

"Ah, well, you know Mary. How are you getting on up there, anyways?"

"Very well so far. After I milked Áine, I had a look at the potatoes, and they're coming along grand. It looks like a good crop this year, Tommy Gilleen will be pleased, last year's crop was poor."

"Aye." Thady nodded. "It's not easy, but you're lucky to have a tenant like Tommy, willing to help you with the oats and the turf."

"I am lucky," she replied sincerely. "He's told me that now the weather's picked up, he's going to start cutting the turf soon so I won't be a 'lady of leisure' for much longer."

Thady laughed. "If there's anything I can help you with, you know where I am."

"Thank you, Thady. I'd better be off now."

"Caitriona?" he called after her and she glanced back at him. "Will you be going up to St Mary's Well next week?"

"St Mary's Well?" She frowned. "The May Day pilgrimage comes around so fast. "Yes." She decided on the spot. "I'll be going."

"You will?" He stared at her in clear surprise. "I just thought that after what happened to John there...You didn't go last year..."

"I know, but—" She felt herself blush. Michael Warner would most likely be there. "I must start living again, Thady. It has been two years now."

"Aye, I know." He took her hands. "I'm really grateful for what you did with Mammy," he said quietly. "I know she must have been like a thousand Mary's all rolled into one but, thank you."

"Well." She fixed her eyes on the ground. She couldn't very well say it had been nothing because it hadn't been. "I'm just glad she had a peaceful end." She raised her head slowly and saw him nod.

"And, Caitriona," Thady continued awkwardly. "You said yourself that it's been two years since John died. You're still a young woman and now you're living alone. I wouldn't mind if you wanted to find yourself a man and marry again, I know John wasn't the best of husbands..."

"Thank you," she replied gratefully. "I don't want to be on my own for the rest of my life. I appreciate you saying that but it will be hard. You won't think I'll be betraying John but there'll be people in this parish who will think I am."

"Idiots," Thady muttered. "I'll let it be known that I don't mind, that you're free to do as you please. All right?"

"Yes," she replied and hugged him. "Thank you, Thady."

"Be careful, though, you don't know how some of the fools around here will react."

"I know, I will. I'll see you at the well."

She walked slowly back through the village. Thady could be a bit of a fool himself at times but he could come out with some very wise words every now and again. At least she had the seal of approval now, she thought happily, as she passed the chapel and approached the Warners' home. In a small field of oats which stretched back from the outbuildings behind the cottage, she caught sight of Michael. Stripped to the waist, thanks to the unusually warm late April sunshine, he was walking though the short green stems. Her heart began to pound. He was beautiful, his chest and back tanned already, and his dark hair bleached brown. Leaning on the wall, her chin in her hands, she ogled him unashamedly.

Michael soon became aware of someone watching him and turned around. Was that Mrs Brady over at the wall? He shaded his eyes and flushed. It was. Quickly pulling his shirt and waistcoat from where he had tied them around his waist, he put them on and walked across the field to her.

"I was just passing." She nodded to him. "And I saw you looking at the oats."

"Yes, they're coming along well," he said quickly and flushed again as he met her eyes. They were very blue. "The sun's helping a lot," he added, struggling to keep his voice calm.

"Yes, it is," she replied and smiled again. His waistcoat blew open in the breeze and he felt her watch him as he fumbled with the small buttons, finally giving up after buttoning three. "My potatoes are coming on grand, too, and Tommy Gilleen will be starting on the turf soon. I help him and his family with their turf and they help me with mine."

Michael stared at her, not really being able to imagine her hard at work on the bog.

"I'm going to St Mary's Well next week," she added. "Will you be going with your brother?"

She was going to the well for the first time since her husband had been killed there. Excitement butterflies fluttered in his stomach and he almost forgot to answer.

"Oh, yes. We'll both be there. In fact, Liam rode out at first light, he's gone around to—" He stopped abruptly and raised a shaking hand to his forehead.

"Gone around to..?" she prompted.

"Both factions," he mumbled. "He's gone to plead with them not to fight there."

"Well, I wish him luck," she said. "You don't have to be embarrassed for me, Mr Warner. I let it be known what I thought the other day. I've no time for men who fight. I can only hope that it will be a peaceful day, with the only activity the prayers and then the dancing."

"Yes, I hope so, too." He glanced down at her hands before doing a double-take. Her wedding ring was gone from her left hand.

"I'll see you there, Mr Warner. Goodbye." She turned away and he watched her walk up the mountain path.

Chapter Three

The people of Doon Parish flocked to St Mary's Well on May Day, where Mass was celebrated. Afterwards, there would be music and dancing, and it was one of the many social events of the summer.

Caitriona was determined to get there early and set off in plenty of time. Leaving the village, she was delighted to see Father Liam and Michael Warner walking ahead of her. She quickened her pace and they turned, hearing someone approach. On seeing it was a woman, both men touched their hats.

"Oh, Mrs Brady, I'm delighted you're coming this year." Father Warner nodded at her.

"The past is buried now, Father," she replied clearly. "It's time to look to the future."

"I'm glad to hear that, Mrs Brady, I really am."

Crossing the stretch of bog and then climbing up a steep slope to reach the holy well field, Caitriona stumbled unintentionally and felt Michael Warner's hand on her arm, guiding her along. She glanced up at him and smiled gratefully. He returned a weak smile and looked away but didn't let her go.

Arriving at the well, they saw people doing 'the rounds' – walking around it while reciting prayers – while at the other end of the large field, stalls had been set up selling whiskey, ale, and bread.

"They're supposed to be coming to this well to pray," Father Warner muttered and exhaled an angry sigh. "I told them all that." Leaving Caitriona and Michael together, he began preparing for the Mass.

Michael pointed to a flat rock. "Would you like to sit there until the Mass starts?"

"Yes, thank you," she replied. "I'm a bit out of breath after the climb."

"Were we walking too fast?"

"No, not at all." She went to the rock and sat down, making room for him to sit beside her. "I'm just a bit out of practice. Except for the market in Kilbarry every week, I didn't get out very much these last few months." She patted her chest. "I'll have to dance later, and try and get fit again. That's if your brother doesn't object." She laughed.

Michael smiled. "No. I'd even go as far as to say that you'll be seeing him have the odd glass of whiskey later on, no matter what he says now. He's not one for the dancing, though."

"Are you?" she asked and he flushed, turning away as a large group of men passed them, doffing their hats to her but she barely noticed them as she waited for his answer.

"I used to be." He looked back at her. "I'm a bit out of practice, too. Would you dance with me later, Mrs Brady?"

Her heart leapt and she gazed into his eyes – beautiful and brown. She allowed him to see her blush and nodded.

"I would be very honoured to dance with you later, Mr Warner," she replied softly.

"Thank you," he replied, before they turned their attention to his brother who was asking everyone to gather around him for the Mass. He took her arm again and they moved forward, kneeling down to pray together.

As Father Liam Warner celebrated the Mass, he stole glances behind him and noted two things. His brother and Mrs Brady were kneeling very close together and almost all the men in the congregation had blackthorn sticks at their side. His heart sank twice over.

Once the Mass ended, he watched as Michael and Mrs Brady returned to the rock on which they had been sitting before. He then turned as the rest of the congregation parted into two distinct groups – the Bradys, in honour of Mrs Brady's late husband – and the Donnellans – in honour of Malachy Donnellan – their leader and champion. Once the alcohol started to flow there would be trouble, he knew it, despite all he had warned them.

He wearily turned back to Michael and Mrs Brady. It was clear they were attracted to each other and he grimaced. He didn't want his brother to become involved with a woman whose name was synonymous with violence and death in the locality. Soon after his arrival in the parish, he'd had to bury three men who had been battered to death by the Bradys. Then, he learned what had happened to John

Brady himself two years ago. Oh, Michael, he thought angrily, don't be a fool and get involved with her, no matter what she says about her hating the fighting. She's dangerous, even if she doesn't realise it herself.

Music and dancing began almost immediately but Caitriona was content to sit with Michael Warner on the rock for the time being. Father Warner passed them without speaking, on his way to one of the stalls. He wore a thunderous expression on his face and she saw Michael stare after his brother in surprise.

"Something else has upset Liam." He shrugged and turned to her. "Would you like to dance now?"

She nodded and he clasped her hand. They walked to where a group of youngsters were dancing a jig and began to dance themselves. Soon a crowd gathered to watch but she didn't bother to look and see if they were Bradys or Donnellans. She hadn't danced in two years and who knew if she would get the chance to dance again with Michael Warner. She did catch a glimpse of his brother, standing a little way off with a glass in his hand and still looking grim, but the priest always looked grim so she turned her back on him and continued to dance.

"Oh, stop." Michael grabbed Caitriona's hand and pulled her away from the dancers. "I'm fit to drop."

The two of them sank down on the flat rock, fighting for breath, and Michael couldn't help but stare at her. Caitriona's blue eyes were shining, her face was flushed, and curls were blowing about her face and neck. She was so beautiful and he wasn't going to wait a moment longer.

Taking her hand again, he led her away from the crowds, the music, and the dancers. They walked until they entered some trees and were out of sight then stopped.

Her expression was so solemn that his heart began to pound even more. He had tugged at his collar in the dance and it and his cravat were slightly askew. His long coat hung open and his hat was pushed to the back of his head. He knew he looked a mess but when would he get her alone again?

"I love you," he told her, letting go of her hand, and waiting for a reply.

She seemed stunned at this sudden revelation and began to pull awkwardly at the skirt of her black dress. She then raised her eyes to his.

"I'm glad," she whispered. "Because I love you, too."

He was so shocked his mouth fell open and he gaped stupidly at her before roaring with delighted laughter. "Oh, thank God." He laughed again. "Thank God."

"I don't know if He has much to do with it." She laughed, too. "But thank Him if you must."

"Thank you, then," he whispered and kissed her.

He had never kissed any woman in the way he did now and surprised himself. Her hands were in his hair, pulling his face towards hers. His hands were on her back, pulling her body against his. His tongue left her mouth and began to blaze a trail down her neck to her cleavage. He was licking the hollow between her breasts, her hands still in his hair, when he felt her tense. When she froze, he quickly raised his head, feeling his cheeks burn. He had gone too far.

"I'm sorry—" he began but she covered his mouth with her fingers.

"Listen," she whispered and he straightened up. Shouts and cries were drifting up to them on the breeze. "Oh, no. A fight's about to begin and they're not even drunk yet, there hasn't been time."

"Liam's still down there," Michael told her as she righted her dress. "I hope he's had the sense to walk away and not try to break it up."

He clasped her hand and picked up his hat, which had fallen to the ground, and led her out of the trees. At the edge of the wood they stopped and stared.

Liam, his hands on his hips, was watching in clear despair as the two factions lined up against each other. Malachy Donnellan, waving a blackthorn stick which must have been over two yards long, was wheeling – walking up and down between the factions, taunting and challenging Tommy Gilleen of the Bradys to fight.

"It didn't take her long to forget him, did it?" Malachy was shouting. "John Brady – the supposed best fighter ever. He didn't seem the best fighter ever to me when I last saw him."

Michael saw Caitriona bite her bottom lip. Why couldn't they let John Brady rest in peace? He gripped her hand tightly as Tommy Gilleen was at last provoked.

"Caitriona Brady has betrayed her husband," Tommy screamed back. "She doesn't deserve to have the name Brady. Her husband was the best fighter ever in this parish. She may not love him anymore, she may have forgotten him, but we never will. Why do you think we're still called the Bradys?"

"None of you have the imagination to think of anything else?" Malachy replied innocently. "You're just not good enough to lend your name to your lot."

"Aragh, you bastard." Tommy rushed forward with his stick, swinging it around his head. He struck out but Malachy met the stick with his own. This was the signal for general ructions to begin and within seconds the entire congregation who, only minutes before had been knelt together in prayer, were beating the living daylights out of each other.

Liam Warner, his hands clutching the sides of his head, turned away from the fighting and caught sight of Michael and Mrs Brady standing at the edge of the trees.

"You could have been more discreet," he accused, hurrying across the grass to them. "Look at them now, after all I said..."

"I told them, too, Father." Mrs Brady tore her eyes away. "I should have known. I should have known that if they're set on fighting – they'll fight. As for betraying my husband." She fought back tears. "He's been dead for two years. Haven't I mourned enough?"

"Some women once widowed never marry again."

"If I'd wanted to be a nun, Father, I would have entered a convent," she shrieked, shook off Michael's hand, and ran away from them.

Michael started to go after her but Liam caught his arm and held onto it.

"Let her go, Michael," he commanded. "It's about time that woman took a long, hard look at herself."

"Herself?" Michael retorted. "John Brady is dead two years but they won't let him rest. She wants to but they—" He jabbed a thumb in the direction of the fighters. "They don't. She wants to move on but how can she?"

"She didn't seem to be doing too badly earlier on," Liam muttered. "A piece of advice, Michael. Leave her be. She's dangerous. I don't want you ending up like her husband."

Tears blurred her vision and Caitriona could hardly see where she was going. She staggered out of the field, onto the road, and walked straight into Thady, Mary, and their children, who were late for the Mass.

"Mother of God." Thady steadied her while Mary looked on coldly. "What is it?"

"Can't you hear?" she asked bitterly. "They're at it again and of course it's all my fault. I hate the name Brady."

Caitriona strode home, slammed the door, and bolted it. She didn't want to see anyone. They all wanted her to be a widow and mourn John for the rest of her life. But how could she mourn him if she hadn't even loved him in the first place? She sank down onto a chair beside the hearth and began to cry in earnest. Raising a hand to her lips, she trailed her fingers down her neck and chest to her cleavage where Michael had kissed her. He loved her. She loved him. Why couldn't people be happy for them? She couldn't bring John back. It wasn't her fault he died. It was their fault but it was clear they wanted her to pay for it.

Chapter Four

The following morning was one of the slowest Michael had ever known. Would Liam never go out? He could only go up the mountain to see if Caitriona was all right if Liam was away. The talking-to he had been given the previous evening was still ringing in his ears.

"That woman is dangerous," Liam had warned him. "She is a danger to you and a danger to herself. Keep away from her, Michael, for your own sake."

Even though he didn't want to admit it, Michael knew Liam had a point. There was a risk in being involved with Caitriona Brady. Both factions in the parish refused to let her husband's memory die. The Bradys in particular, saw him – Michael – as a blow-in from God-knows-where and therefore not fit to be taking up with their former champion's widow. The frustrating thing was that he didn't know what to do about it.

From the far end of the oat field he saw Liam on horseback trotting along the road in the direction of the village. He waded quickly through the oats and climbed over the wall and out of the field. On the road he swore to himself. Thady and Mary Brady were ahead of him, walking up the mountain path and on their way to see Caitriona, no doubt. He sat on the wall and thumped a fist down on his knee in annoyance. When would he get the chance to see her?

Caitriona saw the shock in Thady's eyes when she opened the door to Mary and him. Even Mary was stunned into an unusual silence, taking in her eyes – red and swollen from crying – her limp and undone hair hanging over her face and neck, and her creased and unkempt dress. Mary glanced at the blanket hanging over the back of the chair by the hearth, evidence that she hadn't slept in either bed the previous night.

"Have you both come to tell me how I've been betraying my dear husband's memory?" she croaked, walking back into the kitchen. "You're the first today so maybe I'll listen to you."

"Were you not listening to what I told you last week?" Thady demanded. "John's dead, let him lie."

"But they won't," she replied wearily. "They'll never let him lie."

"Wait, wait." Mary held up her hands, clearly lost as to the jist of the conversation. "What did you tell her, Thady?" she demanded.

Thady sighed. "I told Caitriona that as it has been two years since John died, she was free to look for another husband."

Mary's eyes narrowed. "Well, it didn't take you long, did it? The priest's brother, no less. You went off into the woods with him, I was told. You went off with him into the woods in front of everyone."

"You were told?" Caitriona retorted. "You weren't even there, Mary. Don't think you know what happened because you don't."

"All right." Thady laid a comforting hand on her arm. "I know we weren't there but we did talk to Father Warner and to Michael. Father Warner wasn't very happy-looking."

"What about Michael?"

"He didn't say much but he looked shocked. There was an almighty fight going on."

"Well, it shows that no-one listened to a word I said at the wake." She shrugged helplessly. "I just don't know what to do, Thady."

"I have no objections to Michael Warner courting you, though, I'd say his brother does. The next pilgrimage is next month to Tobar Dhoun. I'm John's brother, I don't fight anymore, so how about I go and talk to Father Warner then, maybe, he can say something at Mass. Everyone will have to listen, then."

"Do you think they will?" she asked in a small voice. "I don't know."

"We can only try." Thady smiled at her, ignoring his wife who was rolling her eyes heavenwards. "I only want you to be happy and if Michael Warner's the man..."

"He is," she replied quietly. "If he hasn't been frightened away."

"Not at all, though, maybe you should be a little bit more careful in future. Michael Warner hasn't lived in the parish very long, people don't know him, and he's refused to be dragged into the fighting. People don't know what to make of him yet. Just be careful."

"You'll want something done before Tobar Dhoun," Mary said shortly. "That fight yesterday was a disgrace. You'll kill someone yet, you stupid girl."

"Mary," Thady warned her as Caitriona's face contorted and more tears spilled down her cheeks.

"Oh, I'll come back later." They all turned to see Tommy Gilleen standing at the door, his hat in his hands, and sporting an almost-closed eye and bruised jaw.

"What do you want, Tommy?" Caitriona asked, quickly wiping her eyes away.

"I just wanted to tell you that we'll be starting on the turf tomorrow, ma'am."

"Oh, you're not going fighting anywhere?"

"No," he replied. "Not until..."

"Next month," she snapped. "I should hit you for what happened yesterday but I hate fighting and you won't be able to see at all."

"But, ma'am?" Tommy began squeezing his hat until his knuckles were white. "What Malachy was saying about your husband and all..."

"What you were saying about me, too. How can I possibly betray my husband if he's dead? Tommy?" she pleaded. "I know I can't stop you all fighting, I was foolish to even think that I could, but can I ask you one thing?"

"Of course you can, ma'am?"

"Change your name from the Bradys. Please let John lie. He's dead these two years. Please let him lie and let me live again?"

Tommy pulled at his lower lip and glanced doubtfully across the kitchen at Thady. Caitriona looked on, her heart pounding. Even Mary waited on tenterhooks.

Thady nodded at him. "Do as she asks, Tommy," he said quietly. "Let John lie. If not for his widow, then for his brother and his family. Change the name. Do it, please?"

"We'll get a fierce slagging next month, Thady..."

"Well, you'll just have to put up with it. I saw you fight yesterday. You're more than able to stand up to Malachy Donnellan. Please do it, Tommy."

Tommy sighed and turned back to Caitriona. It was clear he could see she was begging him and he grimaced.

"All right," he conceded. "I'll talk it over with the lads. I can't promise anything but I'll try."

Caitriona sighed with relief. "Thank you, Tommy," she said. "I'll be out on the bog tomorrow morning."

"Right you are, ma'am." Tommy nodded to her then crept away.

Caitriona went to the chair beside the hearth and sat down, her head in her hands.

"Will you be all right here?" Thady asked her softly. "You don't seem to have been looking after yourself very well."

"Can you cope here on your own?" Mary demanded. "You'll be doing a man's days' work from tomorrow onwards. If you went home you wouldn't have to."

"Yes, I would." Raising her head, she glared at Mary. "This is my home now and, yes, I can cope – I will cope. Thank you for your concern, anyways."

Mary just pressed her lips together and went outside, closing the door with a bang.

"Are you sure, now?" Thady asked softly, kneeling down beside her.

"I'm sure," she replied. "I won't be lonely, anyways, out on the bog all day with all the Gilleens. I'll be fine."

He nodded and she expected him to get up and take his leave but, instead, he stayed kneeling and grimaced. "Caitriona, I called to see Father Warner yesterday evening to discuss paying the dues and he told me that you had already paid it all. Caitriona, you really shouldn't have paid it all yourself."

"Thady, when I knew Bridget wasn't going to get better, I began to put money from sales at Kilbarry market aside – a ha'penny here and a penny there – and I managed to save enough to pay the dues off all in the one go."

"Caitriona, I was going to—"

"I didn't want us to be owing money to the priest – I didn't want anyone finding out the Bradys owed money to the priest – imagine if Malachy Donnellan had found out and used it to taunt Tommy Gilleen and start a fight?"

"I will pay you back, Caitriona," he said firmly. "Every penny."

"You and John would have shared the paying of the dues, so you can owe me half, Thady, and there's no rush with it."

"Thank you," he replied gratefully. "Well." He got up and patted her shoulder. "I'll be seeing you at Mass, then. Good luck."

Caitriona saw him out and closed the door. The Bradys and Father Warner had to listen. They had to. She was surprised Michael hadn't been up to see her. What had his brother said to him? Had he been made to 'see sense'? Had the events of the day before shocked him so much he had thought it would be safer not to get further involved with her? She couldn't have blamed him if that was what he thought but at the same time remembered his kisses and hoped she was wrong.

By the morning, Michael still hadn't come to see her and Caitriona milked Áine before heading for the bog. All the Gilleens were already hard at work. Tommy and his eldest son, Luke, were perched precariously on the edge of the turf bank with their spades. They would cut each sod of turf and toss it to the others, who would lay it out on the heather to dry in the stiff breeze which blew up from the valley.

"I won't be seeing most of the lads until Mass, ma'am," Tommy told her.

"That's all right," she replied quietly. "As long as they heed you."

"I can only try, ma'am."

"Was anyone badly hurt?"

"Ah, no," he replied lightly, leaning on his spade. "Only a few cuts and bruises. Nothing, really."

She nodded briefly and joined Mrs Gilleen and the rest of her children in laying the sods of turf out in rows to dry. It was back-breaking work and soon her back, unused to so much bending over, was aching and her hands were caked in the damp turf. After a while it would dry on her hands and leave them rough and sore where it would crack.

By the early afternoon, when they all sat down with oat cakes and milk, she was exhausted.

"Michael Warner's a handsome man." Tommy's eldest daughter, Kitty, declared, sitting down beside her.

Caitriona blushed despite the muck on her face and Kitty smiled kindly.

"I've seen him look at you for months," Kitty continued. "At Mass and that."

"He is a handsome man." Caitriona smiled and glanced down into the valley. They were sitting a little away from the others so she asked hesitantly, "You don't think I'm being disrespectful to John, do you, Kitty? I'm so confused."

"Oh, no." The girl squeezed her hand. "I didn't mean it like that at all. Lord, no. Two years is long enough to mourn, especially when you could have Michael Warner. He's a bit old for me, though. You can have him."

"Thank you." Caitriona laughed before growing serious again. "When I heard what Malachy and your daddy were saying at the well, it made me feel guilty, and I haven't seen Michael since."

"Why don't you go and see him?"

"I don't know what he'd say if he saw me like this," she said, looking down at herself. "I was hoping that he'd come to see me."

"Talk to him at Mass, then. When you're cleaner."

"I will. I think there'll be a lot of talking done after Mass this Sunday."

Michael was wholly unprepared for the words of warning which Liam delivered that Sunday. Liam glared at the congregation and Michael followed his eyes as they rested on himself, Caitriona, Malachy, Tommy, and everyone who had either caused or had been involved in the fight at St Mary's Well. Most of the congregation fell under Liam's gaze.

"The scene which I had the misfortune to witness on what was supposed to be a happy occasion sickened me." Liam spoke clearly and slowly and the congregation began to squirm. "And the cause." He looked down at Caitriona again, who immediately began to examine her fingers. "Never have I heard such nonsense. A woman cannot betray her husband once he is dead and she has mourned for him. That husband may have been regarded as a kind of hero but he is dead and the woman's life must be allowed to go on."

Michael rolled his eyes incredulously. Liam had hardly given him the time of day since St Mary's Well. Now he was giving him his blessing. Or was he? He was certainly bestowing it upon Caitriona.

"If that woman's life is to go on then her past must be laid to rest once and for all. Her dead husband must be allowed to rest in peace. I will not tolerate this fighting anymore. I know who the culprits are. I saw you quite clearly last week and I have decided that if it happens again I will withhold the Blessed Sacrament from you. You cannot beat each other senseless and then come to Mass and expect forgiveness. I will be watching you all and I will keep my word."

Michael exhaled slowly. That was quite a threat but a necessary one. As he left the chapel he caught his brother's arm.

"Mrs Brady receives your blessing to look for another husband. Does that also mean I can look for a wife?"

"Did I mention you at all?" Liam replied coldly and shook Michael's hand off his arm.

Stunned, Michael wandered out into the chapel yard. Tommy Gilleen and all the Bradys were huddled together in one corner and Malachy Donnellan and all of his faction were in a corner opposite, carefully digesting Liam's words, no doubt. He then saw Caitriona at the gate waving goodbye to Thady, Mary, and their children.

"I should have come up the mountain to see you," he told her apologetically, following her out onto the road. "I'm sorry."

She gave him a little smile. "I was a bit surprised."

"It was very hard for me to get away. I thought you might have come down."

"I was working on the bog with the Gilleens for most of the week and then I was away for a day at the market in Kilbarry."

"Oh, yes. I'll be cutting the turf this week, too."

"Good. At least we now have the weather for it."

"Yes." He struggled for something to say but couldn't think of anything and she gazed sadly at him.

"Well, I'd better be off, then," she said, turning and walking slowly away from him.

Chapter Five

Michael was rooted to the spot for a moment. They were back to the very beginning – snatched conversations about the feckin' weather. He couldn't let her just walk away, and ran after her.

"Mrs Brady – Caitriona?" She stopped abruptly and looked impassively up at him. "What Liam said," he began.

One of her eyebrows rose. "I think your brother made himself quite clear. I'm free to look for another husband but there was no mention of you at all. I don't think he really approves of me very much."

"But I love you," he said feebly.

"And I love you, but we were responsible for starting a fight and I'm terrified that if we start another, someone could die."

"So that's it?" he asked flatly.

She sighed. "Did Thady speak to your brother?"

"Yes, he did – yesterday."

"So you know what Tommy and his faction are whispering about over there, then?"

"Yes," he replied. "Liam spoke to me about your request to change the name from the Bradys."

"Well, don't you think we should wait until we know what they've decided? I don't want another fight next month."

He stared at her. How could she be so calm and collected about all this? "Wait how long?"

"They're obviously talking about it now, so I should know tomorrow one way or another."

"I'll come up to see you tomorrow evening," he said immediately.

"Right, then." She started to walk away again but he picked up her hand, no longer soft and smooth, but hard and rough. He lifted it to his mouth and kissed it. She closed her eyes for a moment, her only betrayal of her feelings. "Tomorrow, Michael," she whispered and left him.

He watched her go until she had turned a corner and was out of his sight. Michael. At least she hadn't called him 'Mr Warner' again. Tomorrow. He should get some answers tomorrow.

Caitriona wanted to cry as she walked away from him but wouldn't allow the tears to come. She'd wait until the morning to see if she should cry or not.

She was up at first light, milked Áine, made butter, and managed to get to the bog before any of the Gilleens arrived. She ran up to Tommy when she saw him approaching with his spade over his shoulder.

"What did they say?" she asked as calmly as she could.

"Well, ma'am." He took off his hat. "I put it to them. Now, you have to understand that we live in bad old times. That secret society, the Ribbonmen, are on the go again trying to control rent rises and stopping evictions. Things are very bad out Killbeg way with houses being burned and the like. And because of that, the County Constabulary are starting to raid houses for arms and it won't be long before both lots start up again in this parish."

Caitriona's stomach began to churn nervously. That last piece of news made her feel uncomfortable for the first time of being alone in the cottage as most of the raids for arms by the constabulary and the punishment meted out by the Ribbonmen both took place at night.

"They shouldn't look badly on you, though, ma'am," Tommy assured her.

"Are you really sure?"

"Ah, yes, ma'am. You charge a fair rent, I've no quarrel with you."

"Thank you, Tommy," she replied. "Well, what did they say?"

"Well, ma'am." Tommy leant on his spade. "I'd be lying if I said that they were happy with what I had to say. There'll never be another John Brady, they said. I'll never be able to match him myself – I know that – they know that – and so do the Donnellans."

"But did they agree?" she whispered.

Tommy sighed. "No, ma'am. They said that we'd be asking for trouble if we changed the name from the Bradys now."

Caitriona's face contorted and she covered her face with her hands. Sinking to her knees, she wept uncontrollably. Both Kitty and Tommy's wife, Maeve, ran across the bog to try and comfort her.

"Asking for trouble?" she cried bitterly. "Isn't that what you and Malachy do before every fight?"

"Shh, now." Maeve put her arms around Caitriona and rocked her backwards and forwards like a baby.

"I don't know what to do," she wept. "How can I try and live a life if they won't let John lie?"

"I don't know, ma'am," Maeve whispered helplessly.

"Why don't you let matters stay as they are until Tobar Dhoun?" Kitty suggested. "Maybe they'll get a bit of sense in the meantime and change their minds."

"You really think so?" Caitriona asked. "I don't want to lose Michael."

"If you go on courting him they might get used to it," Maeve said gently. "I know they don't know a lot about him, and they're a bit puzzled as you've chosen an outsider, and that's why they cry about you in the wheeling."

"Well, I wish they wouldn't."

"I know," Kitty soothed. "Why don't you go home? We can manage here."

Caitriona shook her head. "No, I want to be doing something. I'll be all right." She wiped her eyes and struggled to her feet. "Thank you."

"It'll be all right in the end, ma'am." Kitty nodded encouragement at her. "I know it will."

Caitriona smiled to placate her but her heart was heavy.

She worked hard all day, concentrating on the monotonous sods of turf, then walked slowly home, worried as to what Michael's reaction would be.

Michael waited for Caitriona seated on an upturned bucket outside the cottage. On seeing her approaching, he got to his feet.

"You look worn out," he told her anxiously.

"I am." She opened the door, went inside and sank down onto a chair. "Sit down," she said, pointing to the other.

"Well?" he asked. By her expression, the news wasn't good.

"The Bradys said no," she continued in the same flat tone and his heart sank. "They said that to change the name now would be asking for trouble."

Michael pulled a face and peered down at his hands. That was it, then. They couldn't go on now. "What can we do?" he asked her all the same.

She sighed and shrugged and they sat in silence for a few minutes until she started to rub at the dried turf on her hands.

"Tommy said the Ribbonmen are on the go again and that the constabulary are raiding houses for arms."

"They are? Caitriona, you shouldn't be up here alone."

"This is my home, Michael," she replied firmly. "The Gilleens aren't too far away."

"Hah." He laughed derisively. "A lot of good they've been to you so far."

"They're my tenants and they've been good to me, helping with the turf and the oats."

"But how safe will you be here?" He got up and knelt down in front of her. "You don't know what the Ribbonmen can do."

She stared down at him and swallowed noisily. "Tommy said I'd be safe."

"I wouldn't take any notice of him," Michael retorted, putting his hands around her waist and gently easing her forward until he was kneeling between her legs. "I don't want you getting hurt," he whispered.

"I'll be all right," she protested as his hands moved up her back.

"I'd never forgive myself if you were hurt." His hands moved to her front until they rested just below her breasts then crept up and began caressing them. With a little moan, she arched her back towards him but gasped and drew back from him. Covering her face, she burst into tears. "Caitriona?" he cried softly, pulling her hands down and kissing her tears away. "What is it?"

"I'm sorry," she wept. "But I can't."

"No, don't be." Bending his head, he kissed her filthy hands. "I'm sorry, I shouldn't have done that."

"It's just that." She sniffed. "I don't really know what I'm doing. I've never done this before – courting, I mean – if you could even call it that. I was matched with John when I was eighteen and there was no need for courting. We were married six years and I didn't love him," she added earnestly and he replied with a weak smile. "We did it, but not often, and that's why there were no children, and that's why when you..." Her shoulders slumped. "I'm scared."

Michael held her and soothed her but could have kicked himself. He had never felt for any woman what he felt for her but he shouldn't be too eager.

"I don't know what to do," she whispered, drawing back from him again. "I wasn't very discreet in letting you know I was available. That's why I thought I'd frightened you away, especially after what happened at St Mary's Well."

"I thought you were discreet." He smiled. "That's why I was so amazed when you told me you loved me. I may as well be honest with you, I've never courted before either. So if we're making a right hash of it, who are we to know?"

"But I love you so much." Another tear rolled down her cheek. "And I love you kissing me – I've never been kissed like that before – but I just don't know what to do. The Bradys won't change their name and I've just made a complete mess of it all. I've probably made them want to fight at the wells even more now and if someone's killed because of me...I don't know..."

"Now, listen to me," he said, bending his head so he could look right into her eyes. "You'll have to take no notice of them. If someone's killed, well, it's nothing to do with you. It's their fault for fighting, not yours. You're nothing to them anymore, do you hear me?"

She nodded slowly. "What about your brother?"

Michael hesitated. Liam definitely was a problem. "Don't you worry about Liam. I'll talk to him. Now, are you set on staying here?"

"Yes, I am," she replied quietly.

"Well, at night I want you to bolt the door and pull something in front of it," he instructed. "Close the curtains, too, yes?" he added and she nodded. "Have you a poker for the fire?" She pointed to one lying beside the hearth and he nodded. "Keep that beside you all the time." She nodded vigorously, her eyes wide with fear. "I'll come up here to see you on alternate days. On the other days, you come down to see me. I'll probably be out in the fields, or on the bog, but I have to know that you're all right."

"I will," she whispered. "Thank you."

"I am going to court you, Caitriona," he told her firmly. "And I am going to take you to Tobar Dhoun. To hell with them all."

"Yes." She finally smiled, putting her arms around him as he kissed her lips. "To hell with them all."

Liam Warner saw Michael return to their cottage from the door of the chapel. He rolled his eyes and followed his brother home.

"Yes, I was up to see Caitriona," Michael snapped before he could open his mouth. "And, yes, I am going to go on courting her."

"Have you no sense at all?" Liam raged. "That woman is nothing but trouble."

"She is also frightened. The Bradys won't change their name."

"Oh." Liam was all but silenced momentarily.

"So, I've told her that she shouldn't take any notice of them anymore."

"Will she?" Liam asked. "She always feels guilty when they fight after mentioning her or her husband."

"I hope so."

"Have you heard about the trouble over at Killbeg? And she's up there on that mountain all alone."

Michael pulled a face. "Yes, but I've warned her to be careful and I'm going up to see her every other day."

"The constabulary will be crawling about all over the parish soon, Michael. You should be lying low, not going to check on a woman – the widow of a fighter – who should have gone home to her parents."

"I know." Michael sighed. "But I've given her my word."

Liam glared at him. "Well, on your head be it, then," he snapped and turned away.

Chapter Six

Caitriona did as she was told. She bolted the cottage door, dragged her heaviest chair across the kitchen floor and wedged it under the handle before hauling the other chair on top of it. She then closed all the windows, drew the curtains, and went to bed with the poker at her side.

It was a humid and airless night and she found it hard to sleep. As the night wore on she threw more and more blankets off the bed until she finally slept naked under a single linen sheet, wondering if all this precaution was worth the effort. If the Ribbonmen or the constabulary wanted to get into the cottage, they would.

In the morning and on the bog, waiting for the Gilleens to arrive, she saw her precautions had been necessary. Across the Doon valley, there were three spirals of smoke rising into the sky from the Killbeg upland. Three homes which wouldn't need any further protection.

Tommy glanced across the valley at the smoke when he arrived but he just grimaced and bent and stood five sods of turf upright and leaning against each other. 'Footing' the turf was back-breaking work, but it needed to be done and, turning away from the view, she bent and reached for a sod.

Down in the valley, it was harder to see the smoke but Michael and Liam were starting on their own turf and saw it from their bog. It was proving to be quite a trying morning as neither brother was speaking to the other – until they saw the smoke – that was.

"Look at that." Liam pointed up towards Killbeg. Michael looked to where he pointed and frowned. The violence seemed to be getting closer to them all the time. "What did you tell Mrs Brady to do to protect herself?"

Michael stared at his brother in surprise. "Since when have you been so concerned about her safety? You view her as nothing more than a dangerous annoyance."

"With house burnings as close as that, I wouldn't like to think any of my parishioners were in danger."

Michael raised a quizzical eyebrow before lowering it. Liam was the parish priest, it was only natural he should feel some anxiety.

"I told her to bolt the door and pull something in front of it, close the windows and curtains and have the poker beside her all the time."

Liam nodded. "Good. Then, again, if they're going to get in, they're going to get in."

Michael's heart sank but he knew Liam was right. Caitriona was very vulnerable.

"You're going up to see her again this evening?" Liam asked.

"I am. Why?"

"I still think it would be better all round if she went home but as she refuses to, she will need keeping an eye on. If I'm up that way at any time I'll call in but it cannot be all down to us. I'll go and see Thady and Mary Brady later and see if they'll look in on her, too."

"But she's trying to disassociate herself from the Bradys," Michael protested.

"Thady is still her brother-in-law and should bear some of the responsibility." Liam was resolute.

"All right," Michael conceded. Maybe it was better if there were a few people keeping an eye on her. As long as she didn't object.

"Who will it be?" Caitriona asked when he told her that evening.

"Well, apart from me – Liam, Thady, and Mary."

"Mary?" She roared with laughter. "Oh, I'm sorry, but Mary and I have never seen eye to eye and the idea of her keeping one on me…"

"Liam still thinks you should go home to your parents."

She shook her head. "No, I don't want to. Besides, in a two-roomed cottage with five other mouths to feed, there'll be not enough food nor enough room for me. Am I causing you all a lot of trouble?" she asked quietly.

"No," he replied, though he was only answering for himself.

"I know I must be. I'm sorry."

"Now, stop." He kissed her lips. "It gives me the excuse to see you – as if I needed an excuse."

On his way home, he met Thady and Mary Brady walking up the mountain path. By the thunderous expression on Mary's face, Liam's request hadn't gone down too well with her. He grimaced. From what he knew of Mary, she'd be less than kind to Caitriona.

"She's up there, I take it, Mr Warner?" she snapped by means of a greeting before Thady had a chance to open his mouth.

"Yes, she is. Good evening to you, Mrs Brady." He touched his hat.

"Let me tell you this," she said, walking right up to him and prodding him hard in the chest. "That girl has caused more than enough trouble and I'm going to tell her to go home."

"Mary." Thady shouted, making both his wife and Michael jump. "If anyone's going to be telling Caitriona anything, it's going to be me." Mary just glared at her husband and continued on up the path.

"Don't worry," he reassured Michael. "I'm not going to tell Caitriona to go home. If she can support herself here, then, well and good. Her parents just can't take in and feed one more."

"I know, she told me."

"Yes, well, it's not her fault all that's going on." Thady jerked a thumb in the direction of yet another pillar of smoke on the Killbeg upland. "With all of us keeping an eye on her, she'll be all right. Don't you worry, Michael."

"Thanks, Thady." He shook the older man's hand warmly and watched as he hurried up the path after his wife.

When Caitriona spotted her sister-in-law striding purposefully up the mountain path towards her, she groaned aloud.

"Oh, no – not Mary – not now." She braced herself as Mary squared herself up to her.

"You selfish bitch. Getting half the feckin' parish to look after you. Don't you think we all have enough to be doing?"

"You know full-well I can't go home, Mary," she replied calmly. "There's not enough room and not enough food for me. I can support myself here."

"You can't look after yourself, though."

"That's not my fault. If you really want to scream at someone, Mary, scream at the Ribbonmen. Scream at them," she said, pointing across the valley at the smoke.

"Mary." Thady was panting after running up the path after her. "Hush now, will you?"

"I will not." She turned on her husband. "There are things which need to be said to her and I'm—"

"No, Mary, I am," he commanded. "Caitriona." Taking her arm, he led her into the cottage and shut the door in his enraged wife's face. "Don't heed Mary. I met Michael and Father Warner on the path. They and I will keep an eye on you. Do as Michael told you at night, do you hear me?"

She nodded. "I'm causing you a lot of trouble. I'm sorry, Thady."

"Ah, now." He smiled kindly. "It's not your fault. I'd invite you to stay with us for a while but…" Her jaw dropped in horror and he laughed. "I know. Don't worry, we'll all keep an eye on you."

"Thank you." She hugged him and opened the door. Mary was gone and she stepped out and peered down the path. In the distance she could see Mary striding away. Poor Thady was in for a good ear-bashing when he got home and she smiled apologetically up at him.

"I can cope with Mary, don't you worry." He looked out across the valley at the rising pillars of smoke and sighed. "I've never seen it so bad. Anyway." He turned back to her. "It's not for a couple of weeks yet, but will you and Michael be going to the pattern day at Tobar Dhoun?"

"Yes, I suppose so."

"Good. Well, dance with him there and let everyone see you. The sooner they get it into their thick heads the better and take no notice of what they might say, it's usually the drink talking."

It wasn't the last time, she thought, but smiled and nodded all the same.

"I'll see you soon." Thady kissed her cheek. "Look after yourself, now."

"I will, Thady. Goodbye, and thank you."

The pattern day at Tobar Dhoun drew closer and closer and she grew more and more nervous. Michael came to see her, as did his brother when he had time, and Thady. Thankfully, Mary didn't. Caitriona confessed to Michael that as it had been a month since St Mary's Well, the news they were courting had had time to sink in. Tobar Dhoun would be the test.

There was no question of there not being a fight on the day, even Father Warner seemed resigned to the fact. Caitriona told herself she was not to feel guilty or responsible if she and Michael were mentioned in the wheeling but prayed that they wouldn't be.

Michael was nervous because Caitriona was nervous. He knew how much she was hoping they would be accepted. He was also nervous for himself. He didn't want to be seen as the outsider – the man who was causing Mrs Brady to betray her husband. He needed to be accepted, too. He knew the people of Doon Parish still didn't know what to make of him. Neither faction had tried to draw him in and he knew he was a source of mystery to them. Why hadn't they? What was stopping them? Was it because he was the priest's brother? He didn't know but he didn't want them to know he was wondering. It was his business, not theirs, and the longer he stayed aloof the better.

On the morning of the pattern day, he and Liam met Caitriona outside their cottage and they walked to the well together. She gripped his hand tightly as they followed the many others also making their way there.

At the well, he nudged Caitriona. "Tommy Gilleen's trying to catch your eye."

Tommy took off his hat and walked across the field to them. "I just wanted to tell you, ma'am, that I'm not going to mention anything about you or Michael unless they do."

Caitriona sighed but he knew she couldn't ask for anything more.

"Thank you, Tommy," she replied as he saluted and wandered back to his family.

Michael squeezed her hand as reassuringly as he could. "I love you," he whispered. "Remember that."

"Yes." She leaned over and kissed his cheek. "I love you. Remember that."

Michael smiled as she lifted his hand and began to cross all his fingers. Where was Malachy Donnellan? He searched for him in the throng and spotted him laughing with some of his followers. Please don't say anything about us, he begged, please don't.

Liam noted the blackthorn sticks as he prepared for the Mass. Shaking his head, he turned away from them. What pleasure did these people get from fighting? From beating each other senseless? He glanced at Michael and Mrs Brady, sitting together on the grass. Mrs Brady was very pale and he couldn't help but feel sympathy for her. After last month's debacle, he knew a lot was riding on this fight.

He couldn't help but admire how quickly the congregation divided into two separate factions. One minute they were a mixed crowd but by the next, the dividing line was so very clear. How they could all be praying one minute and fighting the next was another thing which struck him, but certainly not with admiration.

"I meant what I said before," he warned them before he began. "Any man, woman or child whom I see fighting will be denied the Blessed Sacrament until such a time as I think them fit to receive again."

He saw them all nodding but knew deep down that they wouldn't heed him at all.

Caitriona and Michael sat down silently together on the grass after the Mass watching as the crowd flocked to the stalls.

"You go and get a drink if you want," she told him eventually. "Before it's all gone," she added with a quick, nervous smile.

"No, I'll be all right," he replied. "What about you?"

"No, thank you." She tried to swallow but found that she couldn't. She licked her dry lips before inhaling sharply as Malachy Donnellan halted in front of the sitting Tommy Gilleen.

"So," Malachy began lightly. "The Bradys won't be changing their name?"

Tommy's face paled. "No. They won't," he replied.

"Well, I am glad to hear it," Malachy replied sweetly. "It's good to know you've got a bit of sense. The Gilleens just doesn't have the same ring to it. Does it, lads?" he asked his faction.

"Oh, no, no," they chorused, all gathering around their champion.

"Oh, no," Caitriona whispered and felt Michael's arm slip around her waist.

"Christ." He frowned as Father Warner joined them. "It's starting."

"I knew it." The priest sat down heavily. "Maybe you both should go..?" he suggested to his brother.

"No." She quickly leaned over. "Father, if they're going to mention me, Michael, or John, then I want to hear what is said."

"Caitriona?" Thady, with Mary and the children following him, crossed the field to her. "Should you stay?"

"Yes," she replied firmly and strained to hear Tommy's response.

"Look," he was saying to Malachy. "If you want to fight, then don't let it be over John Brady or his widow. John's dead and his widow's trying to live again."

"With a blow-in from God-knows-where," Malachy sneered. "Doesn't that annoy you? That she didn't stay loyal to yous? Maybe she thought yous weren't good enough for her?"

"Well, why didn't she take up with one of yours then?" Tommy snapped. "I'm happy for her – why can't you be?"

"After what her husband did to me and to us?" Malachy roared. "No."

"You're not exactly an angel yourself."

"At least I know loyalty when I see it, I don't go around lifting my skirts to any old blow-in."

Caitriona burst into tears.

"Right." Michael fumed and started to get to his feet, only to be pulled and pushed back down by his brother and Thady.

"Do not get involved," Liam ordered him.

"You fecker," Tommy retorted, getting to his feet. "Mrs Brady's a lady."

"Like your old woman." Malachy laughed.

"What are you saying?" Tommy demanded.

"Only that your wife isn't a one for saying no to a bit of skirt-lifting herself."

"You feckin' liar." Tommy rushed at Malachy with his stick and the fight began.

The small group watching from the edge of the field turned to each other and shrugged helplessly. As expected, the day had turned out to be a complete disaster.

Chapter Seven

The first hour of the fight was intense with ferocious blows being struck on both sides. Liam watched the fighters intently. It seemed that practically all the parish, apart from the group gathered silently around him, would be denied the Blessed Sacrament at Mass on Sunday. At times the noise was tremendous with cries and the clashing of sticks as blows were struck and countered. He listened to the cries, screams and shouts of the participants – normally sane people – here being driven wild by the need to succeed.

As the two-hour mark approached, the fighters began to tire and leave the field to wander home. After three hours, they were all gone and the small group were all that remained at the well. Caitriona Brady's eyes were red from crying. Michael was incensed. Thady and his wife simply stared at each other. Liam himself was shocked by what he had seen.

"I'm going home." Caitriona Brady got to her feet, swayed, and was caught by Michael before she fell.

"I'll bring you."

Liam, Thady, and his wife watched them walk away, their arms around each other's waists.

"I really don't know," Thady said quietly. "That Malachy Donnellan...what he said about Caitriona…" He sighed. "Michael wouldn't have, he seems an honourable man."

"He is," Liam replied, glancing at the departing couple again. Michael was helping Caitriona Brady across a rough stretch of ground, lifting her across the worst part. "Well." He got to his feet and lifted his hat to Thady's wife. "I must be off myself."

"Father?" Thady rose, too, and they walked on a little. "I'm at my wits end. I have no row with your brother at all. He and Caitriona seem to love each other. I just wish everyone would let them be."

"I don't want my brother getting into any danger, Thady," Liam replied. "I see that they do love each other, it's just that Michael – well – I don't want him getting involved in any of the violence."

"No, of course not. Caitriona wants to turn her back on all that, as you heard her say. Maybe that's why she was attracted to your brother."

"Maybe." Liam sighed.

"I just don't see any end to it, Father," Thady said despondently.

"You're not the only one, Thady," Liam replied.

Michael and Caitriona walked home in silence but once inside the cottage she wept.

"Wait until Tobar Dhoun, I told myself," she sobbed. "Maybe they would have found some sense, but no, they're as thick…"

"I know." He held her as her tears began to soak through his clothes. He felt utterly helpless, then he frowned…maybe..?

"I don't know what to do," she continued. "I just don't."

"I know," he repeated, beginning to make up his mind. "Come." He led her outside. "Let's sit out here for a while."

They sat down on the ground outside the cottage. Michael sat her down on his lap and she leaned back against his chest. He put his arms around her and together they looked out across the valley. Only one spiral of smoke could be seen but it was still one too many.

"Where do those poor people go when their house is burnt down?" she asked quietly.

"If others won't take them in, many head for the nearest large town."

"Somewhere like Kilmoyle?"

"Yes, it must be very overcrowded now."

"Were you from there?"

"Just outside the town, but I know what it was like – four or five families in the one house sometimes."

"I'm very lucky, then," she whispered.

"You're very beautiful," he replied and kissed her neck, wanting to change the subject.

"And you are, too," she said, turning and smiling suddenly at him.

"What? Beautiful?" He began to laugh.

"You are." She pretended to be offended.

"All right, thank you." He kissed her again. She had the most beautiful mouth and their first attempts at kissing had been less than successful, showing not only a lack of experience on his side, but also on hers. John Brady really must have been mad not to have wanted her. He let her kiss him and grinned at her, they were both getting better.

The following evening he left the cottage, telling Liam he was going to see Caitriona. He was, but for once she wasn't the first person he wanted to see. He walked down the road in the direction of Doon village and turned onto the townland of Coolmore. At the cottage door he drew himself up to his full height of just over six feet, took off his hat, and knocked sharply. Malachy Donnellan himself opened the door and stared up at Michael in surprise.

"May I talk to you in private, please?" Michael extended an arm out into the yard.

"All right." Malachy followed him outside and closed the door on his staring family.

"It's about Caitriona – Mrs Brady," he began, noting a purple lump on Malachy's cheek, a trophy from the day before.

"Oh." Malachy said flatly. "What about her?"

"What you said about her yesterday, it upset her greatly. She's trying to put John and the Bradys behind her. How can she if you won't let her?"

"Me?" Malachy seemed surprised.

"Yes, you. You kept on provoking Tommy Gilleen, even though he told you that he didn't want to row and fight about her."

Malachy laughed. "That Tommy Gilleen is a right idiot. It didn't take much."

Michael rolled his eyes angrily. "It didn't have to take anything at all, Malachy. Please, I'm asking you, if you have to fight, don't involve her. She always feels like she's caught in the middle. Me, too, I didn't appreciate what you said about me either."

"Mmm." Malachy frowned and folded his arms elaborately. "You are in the middle all right. Not one thing or another. You're quite the mystery man."

Michael knew he was being provoked but managed to swallow his anger.

"I'm just asking you nicely, Malachy."

"Come back when you're prepared to be a man about it, Michael." Malachy turned on his heel and went back into the cottage.

Michael sighed angrily. He would not. He didn't want to be drawn into the fights at all. Well, that was a great success, he thought, and turned in the direction of the mountain.

Paddy O'Dowd, one of the Bradys, was walking home from his bog when he heard a door close. The priest's brother was walking slowly away from Malachy Donnellan's cottage and Paddy quickly ducked behind a wall as he passed. So, Michael Warner, you've finally decided, then. The Donnellans is it, and you courting the widow of John Brady, too. That feckin' bitch. She doesn't deserve to have the name Brady. So this is her way of getting her own back on the Bradys when we didn't do as she asked. You'll regret that, Mrs Brady, Paddy added angrily. You'll regret getting your man to do your dirty work for you. Straightening up, he stamped his foot and headed for the nearest sheebeen. Everyone would be there, they'd know what to do about a punishment.

It was another hot and humid night. Caitriona wearily closed and bolted the door, pulled the chairs over in front of it, then closed the windows and curtains. She again went to bed with the poker in her hands.

Despite the heat she managed to sleep but something – she didn't know what – woke her and she clutched the poker. Wide awake she lay on her back and listened. There was a full moon that night and the light streamed into the bedroom through a gap in the curtains. A shadow passed the window, blocking the light for a moment and her mouth went dry. Another and another passed until she had counted at least six. Her heartbeat was ringing loudly in her ears and she began to pray that whoever they were, they would go on to somewhere else.

When she heard the outside door handle being turned, she began to panic. They started to force the door open and she leapt out of the bed, pulling the sheet around her. She ran to the window but they were already in the kitchen, the bolt and chairs having given way with ease.

The bedroom door opened and she backed away in terror. There were more than six of them – ten at the very least – the poker would be no use as a weapon, even if she hadn't left it on the bed in her fright. They all wore handkerchief's tied over their faces and hats pulled down low over their eyes. From the gloom of the corner she couldn't recognise any of them. All the men crowded into the room and stared at her silently. Then one spoke.

"John Brady was a lucky man," he said and she didn't recognise his voice. "It's just a pity he didn't make better use of her and get a child in her belly."

The others nodded and murmured in agreement.

"What do you want?" she croaked.

The man laughed. "To teach you a lesson," he said lightly. "You couldn't tell John what to do so you've found someone who you can order about instead. That's really annoyed us, what you did, making him go over to the Donnellans. You've really betrayed John now, you bitch. We might have got used to Michael Warner in the end, he was keeping well out of things, but now..." He tailed off and shook his head.

Caitriona stared at him in consternation. She didn't know what he was talking about.

"He's a big, strong man, that Michael Warner," the man went on. "We could have made good use of him, now that we know he's inclined to fight. Tommy Gilleen's a feckin' joke. You could have been the wife of the champion again but now you won't be. Malachy Donnellan will never give way unless someone kills him but he's got a head as hard as rock. So you've made a grand old mistake there, Mrs Brady. Telling your man to go over to the Donnellans when you couldn't get what you wanted from us. Tut-tut." He laughed again.

"But I didn't," she gasped. "I didn't tell him."

"He was seen," the man replied firmly. "This evening, coming away from Malachy's house."

That made her think. Michael had been later than usual visiting her that evening.

"But I didn't tell Michael to go over to the Donnellans," she persisted desperately when she saw him move towards her.

"Well, I don't believe you." The man took hold of the sheet and roughly pulled it away from her, leaving her stark naked. "Christ," he breathed. "You look like one of the angels themselves."

She began to shake as he reached out, took a lock of her hair in his fingers and let it drop.

"That Michael Warner's a lucky man. A feckin' stupid but lucky man." He turned away and jerked his thumb towards her.

"Put her on the bed. We'll see if our friend Michael still thinks he's lucky when we've finished with his woman."

Caitriona was pulled over to the bed, convinced she was going to be raped. But instead of pushing her onto her back, they pushed her onto her front. Two of them held her arms, two her legs, and the speaker pushed her hair up out of the way.

"Now," he said, and she managed to turn her head as he pulled something out of his coat pocket. "I suppose you know what this is?" She strained her eyes in the semi-darkness and saw to her horror that it was a card – an implement for combing wool – with iron teeth. "Lie still now," he said lightly and bent over her.

"No," she screamed. "Please. I'll do anything."

"Good. Lie still, then."

She felt the grip of the men's hands on her ankles and wrists and screamed again as she felt the card being lowered onto her back. It was dragged the entire length of her spine and she felt every agonising inch. The pain was indescribable and when she was released, she couldn't move.

"There now." The speaker seemed satisfied and gave her buttocks a slap. "That should stop you meddling for a while. Anymore, and we do your other side, starting with your face and then those fine tits of yours. You've been warned."

She heard them all leave the cottage before she passed out.

Both Michael and Liam had gone to bed well before sunset as there was another long day on the bog ahead of them. It was so warm they left all the windows of the cottage open for what little air there was.

Some hours later, Michael woke. Liam was snoring away in his bed, but it wasn't that which had woken him, he was more than used to it by now. He raised himself up onto an elbow and looked up at the moon through the open window. It was a beautiful night. He got out of bed, went across the bedroom to the window, opened it further, and took a deep breath. Whoever had said that night air was bad for you was an idiot. He heard a dog barking madly not too far away and recognised it as the noise which had woken him. He was about to return to his bed when he thought he saw something moving on the mountain path.

He quickly closed the window and curtains but peered out through a gap. A large group of at least ten men were hurrying down the path. His stomach began to churn uncomfortably. He watched as they passed the cottage, trying to recognise them, but their heads and faces were covered and he immediately thought of Caitriona. He pulled on his clothes and woke Liam.

"What are you doing now?" his brother muttered sleepily.

"I've just seen a large group of men coming down from the mountain. I'm going up there to see is Caitriona's all right."

"Do you want me to come with you?"

"No, stay there. They've gone now, anyway."

"Well, be careful, Michael," Liam warned.

On reaching Caitriona's cottage, Michael's heart began to pound. The door had been kicked in and he ran into the kitchen. The door to her bedroom was open, too, and he crept across the kitchen, utterly unprepared for the sight which greeted him.

Chapter Eight

A streak of moonlight was falling onto the bed across which a naked Caitriona lay face down. Then he saw her back. From her neck right down to her buttocks, the skin was ripped to shreds. Blood was oozing out of the wound, trickling down her body and onto the bed. For a moment all he could do was stare. Was she dead? Running to the window, he pulled the curtains open to let more light in. Turning back, she was bathed in bluish-white moonlight and certainly looked like she was.

He ran around the bed to her head, crouched down, and pinched her nose. She began to cough and opened her eyes. She stared at him in unblinking horror for a moment, not recognising him, before squeezing her eyes shut.

"Caitriona, it's me, Michael," he cried desperately and she opened them again.

"My back," she whispered. "Help me, I can't move."

He glanced at her legs, they were hanging over the edge of the bed. Reaching down, he began to caress her feet.

"Can you feel that?" he demanded. "Can you?"

"Yes," she whispered and he heard the relief in her voice.

"I'm going to get some candles," he told her, fighting to keep his voice steady.

He ran out to the kitchen, pulling the curtains open so he could see. He found four candles made from rushes dipped in fat and allowed to dry, went to the fire, and lit them all. The rush-lights didn't provide much light but they were better than nothing. He brought them into the bedroom then went back to the kitchen for a bowl of water and a cloth. He sat beside her on the bed with the bowl on his lap and stared helplessly at her back, not knowing where to start.

"Talk to me, Michael," she begged. "I have to know you're there."

"I'm going to try and clean your back," he stammered.

"I was carded. It hurts so much."

Vomit rose in Michael's throat and he swallowed. "I'll try not to hurt you too much," he whispered and began to wipe. She screamed with pain and he winced. She was red raw but he had to clean the wound, he could see pieces of rust amongst the blood. The card used must have been an old one. "I'm sorry." He began to weep, tears blurring his vision, then jumped hearing a cough from outside. Someone was approaching the cottage.

"Michael? Are you in there? It's me, Liam." Michael heard him walking through the kitchen and he stared at his brother as Liam halted at the bedroom door.

"It's Caitriona," Michael croaked and closed his eyes for a moment. "She's been carded. All the way down her back." He held up his hands and Liam's eyes widened as he saw the blood. "I'm trying to clean her but," Michael shrugged helplessly, "she's bleeding so much and I'm only hurting her even more."

"Right." Liam rolled up his shirtsleeves. "Let's see what we can do to help her."

Liam stared at Mrs Brady's ruined back in horror, the realisation of what had been done to her only then sinking in.

"Michael?" she wailed. "Where are you? Who's there? There's someone there."

"It's all right." Michael bent and kissed the top of her head. "It's only Liam."

"Help me," she whispered. "It hurts so much."

"We have to clean her regardless of whether it hurts her even more." Liam lifted one of the rush-lights closer and began to examine what little was left of the skin on her back. It was such a mess. "We're going to clean your back, Mrs Brady," he called as calmly as he could. "It will hurt but there are bits of rust in there and they must come out."

"Then, do it," she said.

"Help me, Michael," he commanded. "Hold the light close while I work."

He picked up the cloth, dipped it in the water and began to swab her back. She screamed and Michael's hands, holding the rush-light, shook. Liam gritted his teeth. The pain she must be feeling he couldn't begin to imagine but he carried on swabbing.

"She's passed out," Michael whispered, smoothing hair off her face.

"Good. At least she won't feel anything for a while." Liam dropped the cloth into the bowl and peered closely at her back. There didn't seem to be any visible pieces of rust left in the wound. "That's all I can do, Michael, the bleeding will cleanse the wound and if there's anymore rust, it will come out then. After that, a scab will form."

It would be a huge scab. They pulled her gently and fully onto the bed, her head on the pillow, and covered her lower body with a sheet found in a corner of the room.

"I'll stay here with her." Michael brought one of the chairs from the kitchen into the bedroom and sat down beside the bed. "You go and find the bastards who did this to her."

Liam shook his head. "They're probably miles away by now. I'll go and wake Thady, he ought to be told. Let her back bleed, Michael, it's the best thing for it. I'll try not to be away too long."

Michael nodded and stroked Caitriona's hair. Why, he raged. Why would someone do this to her? And why her? As far as he knew, Tommy Gilleen hadn't complained about the rent he paid to her for the ten acres of land, so why? He bent over her just as she woke with a jolt and cried out in pain.

"I'm here," he assured her and kissed her temple. "Don't worry, I'm here. Liam's gone to tell Thady."

She nodded and he saw her wince. "Did he get all the bits out?"

"Yes, I think so." He got down from the bed and sat on the floor so that she wouldn't have to lift her head to look at him. "Your back will heal now."

Tears began to roll down her face. "I thought they were going to rape me. Maybe it would have been better if they had."

Michael quickly swallowed the vomit which had risen in his throat again.

"How many were there?" he asked.

"Ten or more but only one man spoke. He did this to me. I don't know who he was – I didn't recognise his voice," she said before he could ask. "It hurts so much."

He nodded helplessly. "Try and sleep again," he told her. "I'll be here, you'll be safe. Try and sleep."

She closed her eyes and within a minute she was oblivious to the pain again. He rested his head back on the chair and closed his eyes but all he could see was the stranger ripping her back apart. His eyes flew open and he decided to keep watch instead.

Liam, Thady, and Mary arrived some time later. Caitriona was still asleep and he went out to the kitchen to greet them. They all crept into the bedroom where Thady and Mary gasped in horror. Michael asked Mary to have a look at Caitriona's back to see if there was anything else they could do. There wasn't, but the bleeding had finally stopped. The blood was beginning to congeal, and in a few hours the scab would form.

"She has no idea who the men were?" Thady asked.

Michael shook his head. "She said only one man spoke, that he carded her, but she didn't know him."

"Could they have been Ribbonmen – strangers to the area?" Mary asked Liam. "She knows most people in this parish."

"Possibly," he replied. "But whoever they are, they're evil."

"Well, she can't possibly be left on her own now." Thady took off his hat and scratched his head. "She can't be moved either, so we'll have to take it in turns to stay here with her."

"Well, I don't know about you," Michael snapped. "But I'm not going anywhere." He turned on his heel and went back into the cottage.

Liam grimaced. It would be hard to move Michael.

"It's only natural, I suppose," Thady said with a shrug.

"Yes, but he's very shocked and I don't think this has quite sunk in yet. She was in a terrible way when I arrived – screaming and crying – he won't want to leave her, but once it has sunk in he will want to find those men. I know my brother and we have to do something," he added firmly.

"Like what?" Thady asked. "We don't know who they are. I'm not saying that we do nothing but…" He shrugged again.

"I know." Liam sighed. "It might be better if I call on some people and see if they have seen the men or know whether anyone else has been attacked."

"All right, good luck, Father." Thady beckoned Michael out of the cottage. "Your brother's going to ask around and Mary and I have to get back to the children, will you be all right here for a while?"

"Yes, I'm staying here," he replied.

"Good," Thady replied before shaking his head. "I just can't believe someone could do such a thing to an undefended woman on her own."

Michael watched his brother, Mary, and Thady descend the mountain path. He breathed in and out deeply. The sun was climbing the sky and across the valley he could see two pillars of smoke.

He went back inside and opened the bedroom window, the fresh air would be good for the wound. Sitting down beside the bed, he leaned over Caitriona's back. She had good healing skin, the scab was forming already, but it looked awful. She seemed to be sleeping peacefully so he got up again and went outside to milk the cow and see to the chickens.

That done, he returned to the bedroom and a still-sleeping Caitriona, sat back in the chair and closed his eyes.

He woke with a jump when he felt a hand on his knee. Caitriona tried to raise her head but couldn't, so he got down on the floor beside her.

"Is my back healing?" she whispered. "It's not throbbing anymore."

The scab was well formed. How long had he been asleep, he wondered, glancing out of the window. The sun was setting, casting long shadows away from the cottage. They had been asleep all day.

"It's healing well," he whispered. "Are you hungry or thirsty?"

"Thirsty. I need to go to the outhouse, too."

He stared at her. She needed to relieve herself, but how was he going to lift her without hurting her or making the scab crack and bleed?

"I'm going to try and lift you up backwards so that you don't bend your back," he told her. "I'm going to lift you under the arms and keep your back straight."

"Do it," she replied and he bent over her and slowly lifted her. He could feel her tense and held onto her until she was in a kneeling position. He then helped her off the bed and to stand. Pulling the sheet from the bed and wrapping it carefully around her, she turned to him with a weak smile. "Thank you," she said. "I was getting cramp, too."

"How is the pain?"

"Not too bad. My back is starting to get itchy."

"That means it's healing. It will get worse before it starts to get better."

"I know." She slipped her feet into her shoes and walked out of the bedroom.

While she was outside, he poured them a mug of milk each and when she returned to the kitchen, he smiled.

"Milk," he told her and passed her a mug.

"Thank you." She pulled out a stool from beside the hearth with her foot and lowered herself carefully down onto it. "I won't be using chairs for a while," she said as she sipped. "How did you know to come up here to see if I was all right?"

"A dog barking woke me up so I went to the bedroom window. There was a moon and I saw a group of men running down the path from the mountain. I thought you were dead," he whispered, kneeling down beside her and touching her face as if to reassure himself that she wasn't. She certainly looked like an angel, sitting on the stool with the white sheet around her and her curly hair hanging down her front. From the back she looked as if the devil himself had been at work on her.

"Thank you for helping me," she replied. "And your brother, too. I was hysterical last night, wasn't I?"

"Don't apologise, anyone would have been. I would have been like a lunatic." He kissed her lips. "Your back is going to heal and you're going to be as beautiful as ever."

"But I'll never forget." She trembled and he quickly took her mug from her hands and put it on the floor. "Never." Her face contorted and she burst into tears.

He went to put his arms around her, remembered, and clasped her cheeks in his hands instead.

"I'm here now, you're safe," he said. "I will never allow anyone hurt you again," he continued fiercely but couldn't help but think that he should never have left her alone and vulnerable in the first place.

"Thank you," she replied, touching his cheek.

"Tell me." He sat down on the floor in front of her and held her hand. "The man who spoke to you – did he have a local accent?"

Caitriona frowned, clearly trying to remember. "Yes," she said finally. "I think he did, but I still don't know who he was."

"Would you recognise his voice again if you heard it?"

"Oh, yes," she said and squeezed his hands but he could still feel hers trembling.

"Do you remember anything of what he said?"

She nodded and took a deep breath to calm herself. "He said I made you go over to the Donnellans because you and I couldn't get what we wanted. He said that you were seen coming away from Malachy Donnellan's house. He said he was going to teach me a lesson for what I had made you do." She began to shake. "But I didn't make you do anything."

Michael felt beads of sweat breaking out on his forehead. "I know you didn't," he whispered.

She stared down at him and frowned. "Did you go to see Malachy Donnellan?" she asked quietly and he began to shake.

He raised remorseful eyes, full of tears, to her blue ones and nodded.

Chapter Nine

Caitriona stared down at him in unblinking horror. Michael covered his face with his hands but she pulled them down.

"Why?" she demanded. "Why go anywhere near Malachy Donnellan?"

"I needed to ask him to stop saying those things about you and John at the wells. I'm so sorry." Tears began rolling down his cheeks.

"Would he stop?" she added. Michael shook his head and she turned away. Her back had been ripped to shreds on account of a failed visit to Malachy Donnellan. "Did you anger him?" she asked without turning back.

"No, but he tried to provoke me."

She looked out the door. The sun had set and a heat mist was rising in the valley. If he hadn't angered Malachy there could only be one explanation. She turned back to Michael. The anguished expression on his face made her want to cry.

"Whoever saw you coming away from Malachy's house must have thought you'd joined the Donnellans – that I'd made you join them as a retaliation against the Bradys not changing their name and letting John lie."

"What?" He stared at her incredulously. "You mean the Bradys did this to you?"

She nodded. "It must have been them."

Michael had to consciously close his mouth. He couldn't believe it. To do this to the widow of their former champion. He bit his bottom lip. It was because of him. Oh, Jesus, why hadn't he left things well alone?

Hearing footsteps approaching, he got to his feet and Caitriona pulled the sheet up to hide her cleavage. Was it Liam coming back? He went to the door, just as a group of six men wearing the rifle green uniform of the County Constabulary stopped outside the cottage. They stared at him then past him into the kitchen. He followed their stares, Caitriona, unable to turn away in time, had her back on full view to them all.

"Can you speak English?" One of the constables stepped forward and addressed Michael in a loud voice, clearly assuming it was the only way to get through to someone unable to speak his language.

"Yes," Michael replied shortly in English.

"I am Constable James Lyons." The man couldn't take his eyes off Caitriona's back and Michael grimaced. "We're – we're—" He faltered. "What happened to her?" Lyons asked. "Her back is ruined..."

"An accident," Michael snapped.

"An..?" The constable eyed him sceptically. "Who exactly are you?" he demanded and Michael rolled his eyes angrily.

"What do you want here?" he asked, his voice beginning to rise.

"We're trying to prevent the Ribbonmen violence from spreading to this parish."

With a hand holding the sheet up, Caitriona struggled to her feet. What was wrong with Michael? Why was he being so rude to the constable? The County Constabulary were trying to stop the Ribbonmen. What was wrong with that? She turned around, the eyes of all six constables were on her, but Michael still had his back to her.

"What happened to your back?" the constable shouted at her. "Was it an accident?"

She opened her mouth to reply but Michael turned and gave her such a hard look that she closed it again and stared at him in fright.

The constable shrugged, clearly assuming she was unable to speak English, and turned back to Michael, who was reaching for the door handle.

"You have an excellent view of the house burnings over there across the valley." Lyons jerked his thumb behind him. "You wouldn't like that to happen here as well, would you?" he added, peering suspiciously at Michael.

"Not particularly," he replied in a cold tone. "Is that all?"

"Almost. Do you live here? We're trying to get our bearings in this parish."

"No, I don't. I live down in the valley, just outside the village."

"Oh?" Lyons sounded surprised and Caitriona saw him look at her again. "Like that is it?" He winked at Michael.

"No, it is not," he roared and Caitriona jumped violently. "I'm looking after her."

"I'll wager you are," one of Lyons' men muttered.

"Since her 'accident'?" Lyons enquired knowingly.

"Yes." Michael began to close the door. "Good evening."

He didn't move away from the door until she heard the constables walk away, then turned slowly around to face her.

"What was that about?" she demanded, not quite knowing whether to be frightened or angry at his behaviour.

"What do you mean?" he replied sullenly. "Feckin' know-alls."

"They're trying to stop the Ribbonmen, Michael. And why did you lie to them about my back?"

He rolled his eyes. "If I told them the truth, they would start searching houses, questioning people, and God knows what else – we'd be really popular, then. I don't want you being in anymore danger."

She sighed and nodded. He was right but he still had been very rude.

"I don't like the constabulary, I can't help it." He crossed the room to her and kissed her forehead. "Let me have a look at your back."

She stood as he moved behind her and could almost feel his eyes on her back. She did feel his hands around her waist and his lips on her shoulder as he turned her around.

"I love you." He kissed her lips. "Your back is healing well. There's quite a crusty scab."

"I know, I can feel it when I move."

"Be careful, you don't want it to bleed again."

"No, I don't," she replied and smiled at his anxious face.

Liam caught up with Thady as he turned up the mountain path, returning to Caitriona's cottage. A few hundred yards along, they met six constables on their way down. All six looked angry and glared at the two men suspiciously for a moment before one spoke.

"Father." He touched his hat. "I am Constable James Lyons."

"Good evening," Liam replied as politely as he could.

"Father, you must know practically everyone in this parish." Lyons spoke lightly and casually. "There is a cottage some way up the mountain. An awfully rude so-and-so answered the door and inside we could see a young woman with the most horrific wound on her back. She isn't his wife and he said that she had had an accident. Now." The constable laughed. "I believe him about her not being his wife – we all have our 'friends', you know – but that wound...she looked like she had been carded."

"Carded?" Liam pretended to look and sound surprised. "Down her back, you say?"

Lyons nodded. "All the way down. It looks awful. She didn't say anything – probably can't speak English – you don't think that so-and-so did it to her, do you? He wanted rid of us and shut the door in our faces."

Thady, unable to understand English, was oblivious to all this and looked on blankly. If he had been able to comprehend, he would have been astonished at Liam and what his reaction was.

"Ah, now." Liam forced a laugh. "I wouldn't know. I'm only new here, myself, I'm still getting to know everyone. But." He grew serious. "What I do know, and what you have to understand, is that the people in this parish don't like you or trust you."

"We're trying to prevent the Ribbonmen violence from spreading to this parish, Father." Lyons sounded a little offended. "The woman could be in danger from that lout."

Anger rose inside Liam but he swallowed it before answering. "I'm on my way up the mountain now. I'll call to the cottage and see for myself. Thank you very much for telling me, Constable. Good evening to you all."

The cheek, he thought angrily. Calling Michael a lout. But, he told himself wearily, as he and Thady continued on their way, I hope Michael wasn't too rude to them. The last thing they needed was the constabulary becoming suspicious.

The two men were pleasantly surprised to find Caitriona in the kitchen and sitting on a stool beside the fire. Michael was buttering a slice of oatmeal bread and passed it to her as they closed the door behind them to keep out the evening chill.

"How do you feel?" Thady asked her.

"Itchy," she replied with a smile. "But well apart from that. The pain has gone. Thank you for helping me, Thady. And you, too, Father," she added, turning to him.

"I'm just glad you're feeling better, Mrs Brady. The constabulary were here. We met them on the way up."

"Yes, they were," Michael said coldly.

"You weren't too rude to them, were you?"

Caitriona watched Michael's reaction as he replied. He pulled a face as he turned to his brother.

"A bit. But they asked for it. When they found out that Caitriona and I weren't married..."

The priest clenched his fists before giving his brother a stern look. She frowned and bit into her slice of bread. What was all that about? That stern communication between the two brothers had betrayed some secret between them. What was it, and why – when she had told Michael all there was to know about her – was there secrecy regarding his own past? She felt hurt and ate in silence for a few moments, before Thady spoke.

"It's my turn to watch over you tonight," he said. "And to make sure you behave yourself."

She smiled but it faded as Michael knelt down in front of her. His brown eyes betrayed nothing, only his love for her, and she felt indignant. Why couldn't he tell her what the secret was?

"I'll be back in the morning." He kissed her lips. "When I've done all the jobs."

"There's no hurry, I should be safe in the daytime," she replied, astonished at herself for not wanting him to rush back to her.

"I know, but I want to be here with you," he whispered. "I love you."

"I love you," she said, giving him a weak smile.

Liam waited until they were well away from the cottage before questioning Michael.

"Just what did you say to the constabulary? Were you very rude to them?"

"No," Michael replied shortly.

"Well, what did you say?"

"I told them what happened to Caitriona had been an accident."

Liam nodded. "And they didn't believe you?"

"No."

"Then, what else did they say?"

"Oh, something about that they didn't want what was happening across the valley to happen here."

Liam stopped immediately. "So they did know it wasn't an accident, even before they asked you. You idiot, Michael, why couldn't you have thought of something else?"

"Like what?" Michael snapped. "I didn't know what else to say, especially with Caitriona there – she can speak English. It's plain to see that she was carded – and it's one of the Ribbonmen's trademarks. It's obvious it wasn't a feckin' accident, but I didn't know what else to say."

"You can't afford to arouse their suspicion, Michael. What about Mrs Brady?"

"Caitriona did question me but I just told her that I didn't like the constabulary."

Liam sighed. "Well, that's the truth at least."

Michael pulled a face. "I don't want to have to lie to her, Liam."

"Have you any idea what she'd say if you did tell her the truth? With a husband like she had..?"

"I know," Michael replied miserably.

"You just can't afford to get into any trouble. Let's just hope that the constable disregards you. Let's just hope that the people here disregard you. You were seen, you know? Coming away from Malachy

Donnellan's cottage. You idiot. What did you think going to see him would achieve? You cannot afford to take sides in this parish."

"I know that," Michael roared. "I know. I know that it was because of me Caitriona was carded, you don't have to tell me, Liam – I know."

Liam sighed as Michael stomped off down the path. How could he have been such a fool? He could have pretended not to understand English – anything to make the constables leave. Now who knows what could happen. Michael should never have got involved with the Brady woman. Because of her, things were going from bad to worse.

Caitriona watched as Thady crouched down at the hearth with some kindling and lit the fire. It was late evening and with only the sheet around her, she had started to shiver. She knew he ought to be told, so she waited until the fire caught and he had sat down.

"Thady, you know Michael went to see Malachy Donnellan?" she began hesitantly and he nodded.

"Well, I think he was seen there and whoever saw him thought he had joined the Donnellans."

Thady stared blankly at her for a few moments then begin to frown in realisation.

"Are you saying that it was the Bradys who did this to you?" he asked.

"Yes."

"I don't believe it." Thady lowered his head into his hands. "To do this to you of all people..."

"Malachy also tried to provoke Michael. It didn't work but they're curious as to why he hasn't joined either faction."

"Yes." Thady raised his head and put his chin in his hands. "He has stayed out of the fights, hasn't he? Don't take this the wrong way, but have you wondered why he came here with his brother? And why they chose to be tenant farmers? And why Father Warner doesn't employ a housekeeper? He can well afford to. With his income, the two of them could have taken lodgings somewhere and not have to work the land at all. Do you know anything about their family?"

"Not a thing, except that they came here from Kilmoyle."

"Would you like me to try and find out about Michael? I could ask at the next cattle fair at Dunmorahan. I'd be very careful."

Caitriona bit her lip. Should she go behind Michael's back and let Thady ask? If Michael found out he would never forgive her, but she had to know.

"Would you ask, please, Thady?" she asked quietly. "But please be careful, it could be anything."

Chapter Ten

Liam looked out over his congregation and sighed. Only four people had come forward to receive the Blessed Sacrament – Thady Brady and his wife, and two others who hadn't been at Tobar Dhoun. The rest looked on rather uncomfortably but made no move to come forward. He wouldn't have obliged them, anyway. He had meant what he had said. When they stopped this ridiculous fighting he would only then change his mind.

"You will, no doubt, have heard of the horrific attack on one of our neighbours," he began, scanning the congregation for a guilty face or ten. Unfortunately, their faces were all solemn. "It was carried out in the most cowardly of ways – at night – when the person was at their most vulnerable. You will also have seen or received a visit from the members of the County Constabulary. Now, unless we want them to become a prominent fixture in this parish, that attack must be the only one and the fights must come to an end, otherwise what will they think of us at all?"

Despite saying that, Liam had a fair idea of what they thought already. Chats with some reliable sources had revealed the constables had been asking questions about Michael –'that lout' – as they called him. It seemed Michael wouldn't be the parish's mystery man for much longer.

"As for the fight at Tobar Dhoun," Liam went on. "It was an utter disgrace, and after all I said. I also said that if there was fighting, there would be no Blessed Sacrament for those who took part and I am glad that those of you who fought have heeded me in that at least. I meant what I said but – adding to it – if the fighting continues, then I will have to seriously consider whether to end the pattern days and pilgrimages in this parish. Unless you want to see the holy wells deserted and forgotten, then stop the fighting."

On his way out of the chapel, Thady Brady caught his arm.

"I'm going up the mountain to see Caitriona soon, Father."

"Oh, good." He nodded. "Michael's up there now milking her cow, but there's a few things he has to do down here, too, today despite it being the day of rest."

"I agreed with what you said, Father. Something has to be done."

"I know." Liam sighed. "I just hope I'm heeded this time."

Caitriona's back healed slowly and itchily and she longed to be able to dress properly again. She continued to wear the sheet around her toga-like, tied at the back of her neck and around her waist, thereby leaving her back exposed to the fresh air and enabling it to heal. At times it was almost unbearably uncomfortable and she would pace up and down the kitchen, wringing her hands, longing for relief, which was of only very short duration. Michael told her of his brother's speech at Mass and she stared at him in surprise. No previous priest had taken such a hard line with regard to the fights.

"Will they listen to him?" she asked, wincing as she felt his hands pass lightly over her back, examining the now flaking scab. If only he would scratch it for her.

"That's the question," he replied and kissed her shoulder. "We have no idea at all." He tied a clean sheet at her neck and helped her to sit down. "It's really healing well now, you should be able for the pilgrimage to St Declan's Well next month." She frowned doubtfully and he added quickly, "That's if you want to go..?"

"I might." She sighed. "No, I will," she decided. "I want them to see that whatever they might do to me, it won't stop me. You're going, too, aren't you?"

"Now that you're going, yes." He bent and kissed her lips.

A month after the attack, she deemed her back sufficiently healed as to be able to dress properly again. She smiled to herself as she slipped into her black cotton dress and buttoned it up. It felt rather strange at first but moving about the cottage carefully, so as not to let it rub, she grew used to the feel of material on her back again. She could go down to the village now as, along with the itch, the fact that she had been more or less a prisoner in and around her own home, had almost driven her mad.

She decided to surprise Michael and, after milking Áine, set off down the mountain path early in the morning with a basket of butter and eggs. Passing the Warner's cottage, she caught sight of him in the oat field and went through the gate. He was bending over, examining the crop, which was slowly turning golden, and she crept up to him. She gently ran her hands down his bare back and laughed as he straightened up with a jump. He gaped at her for a moment before his face broke into a grin.

"You had to be the first person I came to see," she said softly. "I wanted to thank you for looking after me so well."

He flushed and she drew his head down and kissed his lips. To flush like that was an involuntary action and she knew he loved her. She loved him more than anyone she had ever known but knew she could love him even more if only she knew more about him. If only she didn't have to rely on Thady for the information.

"I didn't do much," he said and she laughed softly.

"Oh, yes you did." She kissed him again.

"Is the dress irritating your back at all?"

"No, but I won't be dancing next week. We'll just have to talk."

"Yes," he replied and gently put his arms around her. "We'll find a quiet spot – I hope – and just talk."

She put her arms around him and sighed happily. There had been times when she had feared he would never be able to hold her again. She breathed in deeply, savouring his scent. She knew he still berated himself for going to see Malachy Donnellan but she didn't, she couldn't hold it against him, who could have foretold what would happen to her because of it?

"Will you come inside?" he asked. "And have a mug of milk?"

"No, thank you. Now that I'm out and about again, I have lots of things to do. I'm going to see Thady, then I need to go to Mullen's shop and barter some eggs and butter for a few bits and pieces. Next week,

I'll start going to Kilbarry market again. I'll come down and see you tomorrow. Thady's coming up tonight but I'm going to tell him that there's no need anymore."

"What?" Michael released her immediately. "Me, too?"

"I'm all right now," she protested. "I'll be fine."

"No." He shook his head vehemently. "No, you can't stay up there on the mountain alone after what happened."

"Thady's getting me a pistol," she told him and he stared down at her.

"A pistol," he replied at length.

"Yes, I want to be able to look after myself," she replied hesitantly. She had no idea how he would take the news.

"I want to look after you," he said. "Although." He grimaced. "I don't blame you. A great help I've been to you recently."

"You've been there for me, Michael, when I've needed you," she whispered. "You've been so good to me."

"No, I haven't," he retorted. "It was because of me you were carded. I've been no help to you at all but I don't want you getting a pistol."

She stared up at him with indignation. "I don't think you have the right to tell me what to do and what not to do, Michael," she replied coolly. "Tell me why I shouldn't get myself a pistol so I can look after myself? No-one can be with me all the time."

"What about the constabulary?" he demanded. "They've begun raiding for arms in the parish to stop the spread of the Ribbonmen. If they found a pistol in your cottage..?"

"What will they do? Put me in gaol? I don't think there are many women in the Ribbonmen. I can only tell them that I have it for my protection, that I've borrowed it from my brother-in-law."

"Your brother-in-law," he hissed and rolled his eyes. "I thought you were trying not to have to rely on Thady anymore."

"Thady is not just my brother-in-law, he has been and is a very good friend to me. You couldn't look after me all the time, weren't you grateful that he could help?"

"Yes," he replied, through gritted teeth, she could see. "But I love you, I want to look after you all the time."

"I don't need looking after all the time now." She smiled. "And with a pistol..."

"I forbid you to have a pistol," he shouted at her and she took an involuntary step backwards. "Please, Caitriona." He fought to calm himself. "A pistol is not the answer. You wouldn't want to get Thady into trouble with the constabulary, would you?"

"I could say it had been John's – plead ignorance."

"No," he replied, shaking his head. "They've seen you, they know you've been carded, they've been asking questions. They didn't believe a word I said to them."

I'm not surprised, she thought. "Well, you were very rude..."

"Please, Caitriona, tell Thady not to give you a pistol. I wouldn't be able to rest for a moment."

"He said he'd show me how to use it, or could you..?" She waited for his reaction.

"No." He took two steps back from her in horror. "Lord, no. Caitriona, please..." he begged.

"Michael, when I asked you before why you were so rude to the constabulary men, you said you just didn't like them. Please tell me why and why you're so against me having a pistol?"

"Women shouldn't carry pistols," he replied in a low voice.

"Apart from that."

"I don't want you getting into trouble with the constabulary. You know what they're like..."

She didn't, really, and stared curiously at him as he moved uncomfortably.

"Please, Caitriona, promise me you won't get a pistol."

"It seemed quite all right in your eyes for me to be armed with a poker before."

"Pistols are different. Promise me?"

She just smiled. "Thady mightn't even be able to get me one. I have to go." Standing on tip-toes, she kissed his cheek. "I'll call back tomorrow."

She walked away through the oats with clenched fists. She had no intention of getting a pistol from Thady, or anyone else, but had been curious as to how Michael would react. His anger had surprised her but it had turned into frustration when it hadn't led to him betraying himself. One thing he had betrayed was a great adversity to pistols. She frowned as she opened the gate, went out onto the road, and picked up her basket. She was giving him ample opportunity to tell her his secret but he stubbornly would not. It seemed as though she would simply have to rely on Thady to provide her with the answer.

Mary, washing clothes outside the cottage door, did a double take before scowling as Caitriona approached.

"You're out, then," she said gruffly.

"Yes, I am," Caitriona replied as brightly as she could. "It's been a month and I had to get out and about again. Thank you for looking after me, Mary."

Mary's head jerked up from the washing barrel and she stared at Caitriona in surprise.

"I mean it, Mary," she added. "Thank you. You didn't have to, I know."

Mary reached down into the barrel and lifted out a shirt. "Well, you are family, even though you're doing your best to leave us."

Caitriona ignored that and looked around. "Is Thady here?"

"He's down on the bog with the children."

"I'll just go down and see him for a few minutes. I've some shopping to do."

On seeing her coming, the three children ran forward in delight, shrieking their welcomes. Thady followed them and kissed her cheek.

"It's good to see you out and about again."

"One more day and I would have gone mad." She laughed. "I just wanted to say thank you for helping me."

"Ah, sure..." He tailed off, looking embarrassed. "It was nothing and I haven't really helped you yet."

"About that," she said, and they walked away from the children. "I've just seen Michael."

"And?" Thady asked eagerly and she shrugged.

"I don't know...I keep giving him opportunities to tell me but..." She pulled a face. "Today I told him he needn't come up to the cottage at nights anymore and that you were going to get me a pistol."

Thady's eyebrows rose. "What did he say to that?"

"He went mad, forbidding me to get a pistol, and then pleading with me. When I asked him if he would show me how to use one, he stood back like I'd just hit him."

"Well, I'm going to the cattle fair on Wednesday. If I get a chance, I'll talk to you at St Declan's Well."

"Yes," she replied miserably. "I just hate going behind his back."

"It seems to be the only way."

"I know. But it doesn't mean that I like myself for doing it."

On her way home she stopped at the oat field, put her basket down, and called to Michael. He came to her slowly and when she told him that Thady had thought it wiser for her not to get a pistol and for things to continue as there were, there was unmistakable relief in his face and voice.

Chapter Eleven

Michael watched Caitriona walk up the mountain path before going straight to the chapel where Liam was hearing confessions. He waited impatiently for the last confessee to leave before closing the outside door and leaning wearily back against it.

"Oh, God, Liam."

"What is it?" Liam had begun to disrobe but halted and stared anxiously at him.

"I really don't know how much longer I can go on like this."

"What do you mean, 'like this'?"

"Keeping it quiet, I mean. Caitriona came to see me earlier. She told me she was going to ask Thady to get her a pistol for her protection."

Liam's eyes widened in dismay. "A pistol?" he echoed, walking to a bench and sitting down heavily. "I hope to God you put her off?"

"Of course I did," Michael snapped. "But." He sighed. "God Almighty, Liam, I love her. I hate lying to her."

"But you're not lying to her – you just haven't told her anything. In any case, what do you think she'd do if she did know?"

"I can guess, from what she has said about her husband. But," he went on before his brother could interrupt. "Maybe I should tell her and take the risk."

"No." Liam got to his feet. "Lord, no. Does she suspect anything, Michael?"

"No, I don't think so. But she will soon, I'm sure of it."

Liam sank down onto the bench again. "You'll just have to make sure she doesn't. You do like living in this parish, don't you?" he asked.

Michael glared at him. "Of course I feckin' do – Christ Almighty, Liam..."

Liam moved uncomfortably. "Oh, don't start, Michael, not now. I have the St Declan's Well pilgrimage next week to contend with. There's bound to be another fight."

Michael shook his head with disgust. "For a priest you're so selfish. Don't you care about me at all?"

"Of course I do. I'm thinking of you when I tell you to keep it quiet."

"No, you're not," Michael sneered. "You're only thinking of yourself. What exactly have you been doing in this parish, Liam? Helping people to ease their consciences, giving them absolution and a few Hail Mary's, but when it comes to your own brother..."

He didn't finish but opened the door, went out, and slammed it behind him.

Instead of walking with Michael to St Declan's Well, Caitriona arranged to meet him there. She told him she had baking to do and, despite it being a Sunday, he fell for the lie. She hurried to the well early and, thankfully, the field was all but deserted when she arrived.

"Caitriona?" Thady was seated on a rock waiting for her and his expression was grave.

"It's bad news, isn't it, Thady?"

He nodded and sighed as he got to his feet. "Very bad. I met a Lismoyle man at the fair. He was drunk, so he told me more than he really should have."

"Tell me."

"Come over here." Thady took her arm and they walked out into the middle of the field in case they were overheard. "Liam and Michael Warner's parents farmed seventy-five acres of good land just outside Lismoyle—"

"Seventy-five acres?" she exclaimed before shaking her head. "I'm sorry – go on."

"They had four children but only Liam and Michael survived to adulthood. Even though they had a big farm, their mother took in washing and sewing and sold her butter, eggs, and bread at the market in Lismoyle – anything to make an extra bit of money so Liam could go to Maynooth College and study for the priesthood. This other work – on top of the hard work on the farm – sent her into an early grave, the man told me."

"Poor woman," Caitriona murmured.

"Both Liam and Michael were well educated," Thady continued. "Liam had always wanted to become a priest and Michael had his heart set on becoming a schoolmaster."

"So, what happened?" she demanded. "Why is Michael now a tenant farmer?"

"Caitriona, there's no easy way to tell you this," Thady added quietly. "Michael Warner was in gaol for ten years for being a Ribbonman. He was seen near the home of a family who were about to be evicted. There's also talk of Michael having murdered a constable at or near the eviction, but the constabulary mustn't have had any proof that he did, otherwise he would have been hanged."

She stared at Thady in horror. It was even worse than she had imagined. Michael was a murderer and a Ribbonman. Even John hadn't been a Ribbonman. Tears stung her eyes.

"Father Warner got himself appointed curate in a parish in Ballyannagh so he could be near to the gaol but he resigned when Michael was released," Thady went on. "That was only a month before they came here to Doon. This parish was the first to fall vacant but it would suit them down to the ground – a poor, rural, and mountainous parish – well away from Lismoyle and anyone who might know their history – and Father Warner got himself appointed here and he and Michael found a cottage and land for themselves."

"I love Michael," she whispered. "Oh, what am I going to do?"

"Oh, lass." Thady squeezed her arm helplessly. "I shouldn't have told you."

"No, you should have," she insisted. "Thank you for finding out for me, I knew there was something. Little wonder they've been keeping themselves to themselves."

"Aye." Thady nodded. "Michael seemed such a nice man for you. Oh." He turned and she followed his gaze. "Here's the man himself."

Michael waved and started across the field towards them, leaving Father Warner at the well. "Caitriona." He greeted her with a kiss on her cheek. "Thady." He shook his hand warmly.

"How are you?" Caitriona asked, forcing herself to slip her hand into his.

"Busy – working hard on the bog – I've it nearly all footed now."

"Good," she replied simply, turning as more and more people arrived and the stalls were set up.

"Here comes trouble," he said as Malachy Donnellan walked onto the field, blackthorn stick in hand.

"Well, I'd better be off back to Mary and the children." Thady touched his hat to her before walking away.

"When the Mass is over, do you want to go for a walk?" Michael asked. "To get away from the fight, I mean?"

Caitriona glanced up at him, wondering if she should go off alone with him, shocking herself at such a thought. He had never intentionally hurt her so she nodded.

"Yes, I'd like that."

"Good. Come on, Liam's ready to begin."

She was so shocked at Thady's news she could hardly concentrate on the Mass. What was she going to do? She really shouldn't have anything more to do with Michael, it would be like John all over again except for one thing, she loved Michael, she couldn't help it.

When the Mass ended and the crowd began to separate, Michael took her hand and they walked away. He led her into a small wood where they sat down. She watched nervously as he pulled a package out of one coat pocket and a bottle out of the other.

"Bread," he explained as he unwrapped the package revealing two slices thickly smeared with butter. "Milk," he added, holding up the bottle. "I thought we might get hungry."

"Oh." She peered guiltily at the little meal on his lap. "I should have brought something with me, too."

"You brought yourself," he said, handing her a slice of bread and the bottle. "You didn't get a pistol from Thady, did you?"

He said it so casually that she jerked her head up and stared at him. She met his eyes but she couldn't read anything in them.

"No, I didn't," she replied just as casually and watched his reaction.

"Good," he replied with clear relief. "You don't need a pistol. I'll look after you."

She gave him a weak smile and began to eat and drink. An hour ago she would have been comforted by his words. Now they made her stomach churn. She passed the bottle back to him and struggled to finish the bread.

Michael moved behind her, leant back against a tree and gently eased her back against his chest. Wriggling a little to get comfortable, her breasts came to rest in his hands. She closed her eyes as he caressed her, his fingers seeking out her nipples. She tried to block everything out and enjoy his hands on her body but she couldn't. She couldn't now she knew those hands had killed someone and she sat up abruptly, startling him.

"Don't do that," she cried and struggled to her feet.

"What?" He gaped up at her in astonishment. "What is it? Was I hurting you?"

"No," she replied, her face contorting. "I have to go." She stooped to pick up her shawl before running away from him as fast as she could.

Caitriona ran home, not stopping once. Inside the cottage, she sank onto a chair, gasping for breath. All her feelings of security, safety – that Michael would look after her – were gone. The blood on his hands when she had been carded would not have been the first and she swallowed the rising vomit in her throat. What was she going to do? The first man she had ever loved and he was a murderer.

When she heard a knock at the door she expected it to be Michael and debated whether to ignore it. On finally opening it, she saw an anxious Thady with the three children.

"I'm sorry, Caitriona, but Mary's caught a chill and the walk to the well and back has made it worse – it's gone on her chest – and she's gone to bed. Could you look after these three scallywags for a few days? I'd do it, only Mary's not in the best of humour and I thought it best to let her have as much peace and quiet as possible to recover."

'Not in the best of humour'. Poor Thady, an ill Mary's temper must be dreadful altogether. She smiled, the children would keep her mind off Michael for the time being.

"Of course I can."

"Great." The three children rushed past her into the kitchen, dumping a bag down in the middle of the floor.

"Behave yourself for Caitriona," their father warned them. "I'll be up again in a couple of days. Thanks very much," he added, turning back to her. "There's a few bits and pieces in the bag. Don't take any cheek and give them some jobs to do to keep them out of trouble."

"I will." She laughed. "We'll have great fun."

"How are you?" he asked and her smiled faded. "I didn't see you again at the well."

"No." She looked down at her feet. "I left."

"You left Michael there?"

"Yes."

"Be careful," Thady whispered and her head jerked up. "If you start acting differently towards him or refuse to see him, he might suspect you know something."

"But what can I do?" she replied quietly. "I love him but I hate him, too, for being a murderer."

She ended on a whisper and her eyes filled with tears. She couldn't help loving him far more than she hated him and that just made it worse.

"Ah, lass." Thady squeezed her hands. "I've made you upset."

"No." She shook her head. "You haven't. I just wish that he had told me, not you."

"Maybe he's afraid of losing you."

"Probably, but he should have told me, anyway."

"I shouldn't have told you," Thady said sadly.

"You should," she insisted. "It's just that I don't want to try and behave as if I don't know. That's why I couldn't be with him today."

"You can't go on avoiding him."

"I know. I'll just—" She pulled a face. "I'll just have to keep on giving him the chance to tell me. If not," she saw by Thady's expression that whatever this was going to be, it was going to be the most likely. "Then, I'll have to tell him that I know. I won't tell him how or why, you needn't worry, Thady."

"I hope it won't come to that."

"So do I," she replied.

She had never been more happy to have company in the cottage. The three children soon behaved as they had lived there all their lives. Caitriona had to decide quickly where they were all going to sleep.

"You're to have my bed," she told them and they followed her into the bedroom. "It's the biggest, I'll sleep out in the kitchen in the hag bed."

"There's some bread and butter and milk in the bag," Maire, the eldest, told her.

"Thank you." Caitriona smiled and they all went back out to the kitchen. "We're going to have a great time, aren't we?"

"Yes."

"Is there anything we can help with?" Maire asked.

"Well." Caitriona glanced out the door to the last few sods of the previous year's turf. "Tommy Gilleen said he would be delivering the turf tomorrow and I was going to spend the next couple of days building the rick..."

"Oh, we'll help when it comes." Cormac, the youngest, answered for all of them and she gave him a grateful smile.

The children enjoyed the change of scenery, even though Caitriona would often catch them looking across the valley to the smouldering fires on the Killbeg upland. It was hard to get them to go to bed but once they were there they all fell fast asleep. She went to bed soon after but lay awake, not because of the strange bed, but because her mind was in turmoil.

Michael was a Ribbonman and a murderer. Like John, he had killed someone. But why did she still love him? She had sworn never again to be in any way involved with a violent man and here she was...she grimaced in despair into the darkness. Part of her was relieved he had not followed her home but the rest of her yearned for him to come and touch her in that way again.

Tommy Gilleen was true to his word and his donkey and cart stopped outside the cottage shortly after they had eaten their breakfast.

"I'm glad to see you out and about again, ma'am," he said, touching his hat before jumping to the ground.

"I'm glad to be out and about again," she replied and extended a hand into the cottage. "Please come inside, Tommy, I need to ask you something."

He followed her into the kitchen and she closed the door so the children wouldn't hear them.

"If you know which of the Bradys carded me, I want you to tell me now," she said and his eyes widened.

"The Bradys, ma'am?"

"Don't you dare tell me that it wasn't one of the Bradys, Tommy," she snapped.

"But, ma'am—"

"Did you know of a plan to card me, Tommy?"

"No, I did not," he replied adamantly. "And if it was some of the Bradys – or men acting in the name of the Bradys then—" His shoulders slumped. "I swear to God that I don't know who they are. I didn't ask for you to be carded, know who carried it out, or know anything about it."

He clearly hated having to admit this and she grimaced. "Do you suspect anyone?"

"No, ma'am, I don't. And I know," he added before she could speak. "This makes me look weak. John would have known if anyone had gone behind his back and dealt with them."

"John is dead," she shouted and Tommy flushed. "Listen to me – let John lie – you don't fight for him anymore – or for me. If you don't want to be seen as weak, then don't allow Malachy to provoke you anymore – rise above his taunts – please, Tommy?"

"I can only try, ma'am," he said quietly, and opened the door. "Let's off-load this turf, I have mine to cart home today, too."

Soon there was a huge heap of turf outside the cottage and she and the children waved Tommy off.

"This is very good of you," she said, crouching down to get at the turf as her back was still rather tender and she didn't want to be straightening up and bending down all the time. "I know you'll soon be building your own rick."

"I'm glad we can help – you shouldn't be doing it all on your own so soon after being ill," Siobhan replied. "And the sooner we're finished, the sooner we can play."

They were about to stop for something to eat when Cormac poked her in the side and pointed. Caitriona straightened up slowly and carefully and shaded her eyes against the sun. Her heart sank. Michael was striding purposefully up the mountain path towards her.

Chapter Twelve

Michael couldn't put it off any longer. He had to find out what had made Caitriona run away from him. The tone of her voice had been one of fear and she had run away as fast as she could. He had to find out why. Nearing the cottage, he slowed his pace. Who were those children? Then he saw they were the Brady children and groaned. What were they doing up there with her?

He forced a smile as he stopped beside them all. "You're all working hard."

"We're helping Caitriona build the rick of turf," Cormac replied. "We're staying here because Mam's sick."

"Not very sick, I hope?"

"Ah, no, just a bad cold."

"Well, I hope she's well again in no time," he said, raising his eyes from the boy to Caitriona. She looked flushed, maybe it was exertion from the work. Her eyes were firmly on her hands, rubbing them together in an effort to rid them of turf crumbs. She didn't seem to want to look at him. "Caitriona." He greeted her in a low voice.

She raised her eyes reluctantly. "Hello, Michael," she said simply.

He saw she was going to make no effort to ask him into the cottage so they could talk in private. The children were staring curiously at them and he moved awkwardly.

"I just came…" He cleared his throat. "I thought you might be ill after—"

"Yes," she interrupted. "I didn't feel well."

"You shouldn't be out here working."

"I'm fine now," she replied and scowled as she looked down at her hands again.

He stared helplessly at her. There clearly was something wrong and he racked his brains for an idea as to how he could get her inside and speak to her in private.

"I'm roasted after the climb," he announced. "Could I have a drink of milk, please, Caitriona?"

Her head jerked up and she hesitated and glanced at the children. Was she hoping they wanted some, too? Thankfully, they didn't and began to return to their work. Caitriona pressed her lips together in obvious irritation and walked towards the cottage.

Once inside he quickly closed the door and leaned back against it.

"What is wrong, Caitriona?" he asked calmly.

She spun around, a mug in her hand. "What do you mean?"

"Exactly what I say. What is wrong?"

"Nothing."

"There is. Tell me."

She turned away, poured milk into the mug, and handed it to him.

"Things are moving too fast, Michael. I'm not used to this. I need time to get used to being courted. Besides, I know little or nothing about you."

He frowned and gripped the mug with both hands. "Yes, you do. You know I'm from Lismoyle and that I have been a farmer all my life..."

"You know everything there is to know about me. Those two things – they aren't enough. Where are the rest of your family? Why did you move here with your brother?" Her voice rose and became more impassioned as she spoke.

He drank and put the mug down on the table.

"There isn't much to tell. My parents are dead. Liam and I are their only surviving children. We moved here – well, he was offered the parish – and I decided to come, too. He is my only living relative."

She waited, as if expecting him to continue. When he didn't, she spoke.

"I would prefer if you didn't court me for a while, Michael. It will give everyone time to think."

"Think?" he replied incredulously. "People in this parish don't know how to think – only fight."

Caitriona raised her chin stubbornly. "I can't see you for a while, anyway, because of the children."

"Well, isn't that convenient."

"They are my nieces and nephew."

"And what the hell am I to you?" he demanded. "I love you."

To his horror, she hesitated again before answering.

"I love you, too," she mumbled. "But I mean what I say."

"Well, fine." He strode to the door. "You're so used to being looked up to as the wife of a champion that you want me to be at your beck and call. Well, let me tell you this; I'm going to be at nobody's beck and call, do you hear me? I'm not a dog that you whistle and I come running. I can't live like that and I feckin'-well won't."

He flung the door open. The three children were staring at him again, clearly frightened at having heard raised voices. He glared at them before striding away.

He stomped angrily back down the path to the village. If she hadn't wanted to see him again, why hadn't she come straight out with it? He was hurt – which made him furious – and he slammed the cottage door shut, making Liam jump.

"What is it?" Liam demanded, closing his bible and getting up from the table. He had been flicking through it, clearly trying to come up with a suitable text on which to base his next homily.

"Caitriona doesn't want me to court her for a while."

"Oh? Why?"

"I don't know. I've done nothing to make her consider wanting to end our courtship."

"That's women for you," Liam said flatly.

"What?" Michael gave him an 'as if you would know' look.

"Maybe it's for the best," Liam went on. "What if she had found out?"

"How?"

"I don't know. That's why I'm saying it is probably for the best."

"But you've never known what its like to be in love." Michael threw his arms up into the air in despair. "I'm going to tell her," he decided, walking towards the door. "What harm can it do now?"

"No." Liam ran after him, grabbing his shoulders, and pinning him to the wall. Despite being smaller and slighter, Liam managed to take him completely by surprise. "Don't you dare tell her. Have you any idea what could happen if it became known? We'd have to move again. You'd never see that damned woman again – ever. Do you want that?" he demanded and Michael grimaced, shaking his head. "Well, stop behaving like an ass and prepare our dinner." Liam let him go and returned to his bible.

Caitriona watched Michael descend the mountain path, a lump rising in her throat. She closed the cottage door so the children wouldn't see her cry and sat down at the table with her head in her hands. Why hadn't he told her? She had given him yet another opportunity to. What did she have to do? Tell him she did know? What would that do to him? He would know she had gone behind his back, that's what. He had stormed off with little or no intention of coming back as it was. He was in such a rage, maybe it was just as well...

"Caitriona?" Maire's frightened voice made her jump, she hadn't heard the door open. "Did you row with Mr Warner?"

"Yes, I did," she replied, wiping her eyes. "Come on. We need to eat." She got up, squeezed the girl's shoulder, and went to the fire.

Thady called the next morning and his jaw dropped in shock when he saw the dark circles under her eyes. She had been shocked herself when she peered into her small hand mirror and had pinched her cheeks hard in an effort to force some colour into them before the children saw her.

"Oh, Lord, Caitriona, I'm sorry. Were the children too much for you?"

"No," she replied truthfully. "They've been great. We've just finished building the rick of turf. I just haven't been sleeping very well, that's all."

"I see. Well, the main reason I came up was to tell you that Mary's a lot better and the children will be able to come home tomorrow. Thanks for having them."

"It was nothing, Thady."

"Another thing," he added, lowering his voice. "I saw Michael just now in the village and he ignored me."

"I'm sorry, I told him I didn't want him to court me for a while," she said miserably. "It didn't go down very well."

"You rowed?"

"Yes," she whispered. "I don't think he's coming back."

"Oh, lass." Thady took her arm, led her inside and closed the door on the playing children. "I'm sorry to hear that. But it might be for the best."

"Really," she replied flatly.

"He doesn't think you know, does he?"

"No, I don't think so."

"Good." Thady both looked and sounded relieved. "We don't know what might happen if he did find out you knew."

"I know," she replied, remembering how angry he had been.

"You'll meet someone worthy of you, lass, I know it." Thady smiled kindly at her.

"No, I won't." She was firm. "I'm having nothing to do with any of the fools around here – none of them."

"Caitriona—" He tried to calm her.

"No," she cried, waving her arms about in sheer frustration. "You can tell them all – all those idiots – that they've won. John Brady's widow will be mourning him for the rest of her life, even though she loves another man."

Thady winced and Caitriona immediately regretted her words.

"I'm sorry, I shouldn't have said that."

He shook his head. "No, lass, I know. It's so damned unfair. I'm so sorry for all your trouble. If only I hadn't told you."

"But I'd still have suspected and I would probably have found out some other way. No, please don't regret telling me, Thady, I wanted you to."

"All right." He squeezed her arm. "I'll take the children home after Mass in the morning and give you some peace and quiet again."

Caitriona pulled a face, not sure whether she wanted some peace and quiet again.

As it was the children's last night in the cottage, Caitriona wanted to make it a memorable one. She cooked oatcakes on the griddle pan over the fire for supper then they went outside and played hide and seek. It was starting to get dark – usually long past the children's bedtime – when they finally went inside and she closed the door to keep the midges and moths out.

"Do we really have to go to bed now?" Cormac moaned.

"You'll never get up for Mass if you don't." She smiled at his disappointed face. "Your daddy is bringing you home afterwards."

"We've had a great time here, Caitriona. Thank you for having us."

She couldn't help but laugh, knowing that he was trying to molly-coddle her into letting them stay up a bit longer and almost succeeding.

"Look," she decided. "You go and get into bed and I'll be there in a few minutes and I'll tell you a story my grandmother used to tell me."

"Great." The three children scuttled off to the bedroom.

She laughed again before bolting the door, drawing the curtains, and getting undressed. She was seated on the hag bed in her nightdress and brushing her hair when she was shouted at to hurry up from next door. She reached for her shawl and went into the bedroom. The three children were snuggled up together in the bed waiting eagerly for her. She sat cross-legged at the end of the bed while telling them the story, marvelling at the three enraptured faces in front of her. When she finished and prepared to go back out to the kitchen, Maire grabbed her arm.

"Will you stay here with us?" she pleaded.

"With three big lumps like you? Will there be room?" she teased.

"Yes." They all rolled over, leaving a big space in the centre of the bed.

"Well, it looks as if you're not as big as I thought you were." She pulled off her shawl and crawled into the bed. "Now, no talking," she commanded lightly. "Or we'll never get up for Mass in the morning. It's very late."

"All right," they chorused.

She did end up answering one or two questions then had to pretend to be asleep otherwise it would have gone on all night. She eventually did sleep and slept dreamlessly until she saw Michael. At first she couldn't see what he was doing but it then became clearer. He was bashing another man's head off a rock. The man's blood and brains were splattering all over the rock and all over Michael's face, hands, and clothes.

She woke with a jump but immediately lay still, fighting to control her laboured breathing in case she woke the children. She turned slowly onto her side. Dawn was breaking and grey light was coming in through a gap between the curtains and the wall. She closed her eyes and tried to sleep again but her eyes flew wide open a second time. What was that noise? The three children were still asleep beside her, it wasn't them, but there was definitely someone outside.

A shadow then passed the window. Then another and another.

"Oh, no," she whispered. "Not again."

Chapter Thirteen

The sound of a fist being banged on the cottage door woke the three children.

"What is it?" Cormac began to wail.

"I'll just go and see." She kissed his cheek, trying to comfort him, then reached for her shawl and put it around her shoulders. She went nervously out into the kitchen, jumping violently as, again, a fist was banged on the door.

"If you don't open this door, we'll have to force it," a stranger's voice commanded in English.

"Who are you?" she stammered, also in English. "There are children in here."

"County Constabulary," came the swift reply. "Open the door."

With shaking hands, she unbolted the door then was forced to jump back as the door was flung open. Five constables burst into the kitchen, one opened the curtains to admit more light, while the others looked her up and down.

"Name?" one demanded, as the others went into the bedroom.

"Caitriona Brady," she replied as the children screamed, ran out of the room, and clung to her.

"Brady?" he repeated sharply and Caitriona recognised him as Constable James Lyons, whom Michael had been rude to. "Anything to John Brady, the fighter?"

"His widow," she whispered.

"I see." A smirk spread across Lyons' face. "So that lout here before was just a 'friend'?"

"What do you want?" She fought to control her voice. "How dare you burst in here with children about."

"But you let us in, Mrs Brady." He smiled infuriatingly. "Are they yours?"

"No, they're my nieces and nephew."

"Well, I am glad to hear that you can actually speak English." He began to wander around the kitchen, only stopping at the chair beside the fire to run his fingers over her clothes. "You seemed a bit tongue-tied before. Maybe it was your 'accident'?"

"Yes."

"Who did it to you?" He turned on her, she shrank back, and one of the children screamed again. "Did he card you? That lout? Did he?"

"No," she cried, stroking the children's hair. "No, he didn't."

"Then who was it?"

"I don't know."

"Oh, come now, Mrs Brady. This parish lives in each other's pockets – you must know who it was."

"Then you aren't doing your job properly at all," she shouted, startling him. "If you were, you would know that this parish is divided in two by faction fighting. Why do you think I'm a widow?"

"So you have enemies, Mrs Brady?"

"It would seem so."

"And why do you think that is?"

"You definitely aren't doing your job properly," she sneered, as the four other constables began to search the kitchen. "I don't have a pistol," she told them but they ignored her and opened the doors in the bottom of the dresser, pulling all the contents out on to the floor. "I should have, though."

"Is that a threat, Mrs Brady?"

"To protect myself, Constable. I need something."

"You didn't seem to be doing too badly protection-wise, the last time we met," he replied lightly before turning to his colleagues. "Anything?"

"No," one answered, throwing a blanket back onto the hag bed.

"Good." The constable smiled at her. "Let's keep it that way, shall we, Mrs Brady?" he added, turning to go.

"It's not pistols you should be looking for," she shouted after them. "It's sticks – blackthorn sticks – hazel sticks – look for them."

"We weren't told to look for them," he called back over his shoulder. "Thank you for your co-operation, Mrs Brady."

She slammed the door after them and the children burst into tears.

"It's all right now," she said, kneeling down and hugging them tightly to her. "They're gone. I'll bolt the door." She was prevented from doing so for a good five minutes as the three children clung to her, wailing loudly. "They're gone," she repeated, reaching over and sliding the bolt into place. "Now – look – they can't get in again." Even so, the children still clung to her. Cormac was shaking uncontrollably. "Do you want some warm milk?" she asked, knowing it would be too much to ask them to go back to bed just yet. "Then, I'll tell you another story?" They nodded.

"I'll tidy up the mess." Maire wiped her eyes and went to the dresser.

Caitriona sat the two younger children down on the hag bed, rattled the red-hot ashes in the hearth and threw on some turf. She poured some milk into a pot and hung it over the fire to heat then sat down on the bed, hugged the children to her again, and told them the cheeriest story she could think of. After the warm milk and, despite their protestations that they wouldn't be able to, they went into the bedroom and slept.

Caitriona only dozed, she was too shaken and angry to sleep deeply. The constabulary should be looking for blackthorn sticks and trust them to raid her house with the children there. She finally did sleep but woke to find the sun high in the sky – they were going to be late for Mass.

"Hurry now, collect all your things, your Daddy's taking you home afterwards. I'm sorry you had such a fright."

"It's not your fault." Maire hugged her. "Really, it isn't."

They hurried down the mountain path to the village, only to find that Mass was already well under way.

When Michael heard the chapel door open, he saw Liam turn to face the congregation and roll his eyes to heaven, clearly thinking that if people couldn't come to Mass on time, they shouldn't come at all. Behind him, he heard feet walking up the aisle, a child bursting into tears then a fevered outbreak of whispering. This final interruption was too much for Liam.

"Please, Mrs Brady," he cried irritably. "The Mass has started."

Michael jumped at the mention of her name. Turning around, he peered across the gloom of the chapel to where the women and children sat. Caitriona's face was grey and the three children were crying and clinging to their mother.

"I'm sorry, Father," she said. "But the children and I had a fright early this morning. The County Constabulary raided my house for arms."

Michael was shocked. No wonder she looked awful. Glancing at Liam, he saw his brother sigh. That was different.

"Were any of you hurt, Mrs Brady?"

"No, Father, we were just shocked and frightened. I'm very sorry for being late and interrupting you."

As the Mass drew to a close, Michael began to edge to the end of his pew, wanting to be one of the first out of the chapel so he could speak to her. Every few minutes he could feel her eyes on him and he knew she was going to try and leave quickly, too.

Infuriatingly, she managed to be first out of the chapel and not him, but as he queued to leave, he saw Thady, Mary, and the children race out after her into the chapel yard.

"You can't run off like this." Thady grabbed her arm and Michael silently thanked him for stopping her. "Thanks for looking after the children last night, it must have been terrible."

"It was," she replied, with a desperate glance to the chapel door.

"Bolt the door at night," Thady warned.

"I will." She turned to go and was at the gate by the time Michael was outside. She began to run up the road to where it petered out and the mountain path began but he ran after her and seized her arm.

"Stop, Caitriona. Wait, please."

"I must get home," she protested.

"Last night," he began hesitantly. "The constabulary didn't do anything to you?"

"No, they didn't, the children were there."

"That doesn't always stop them. Please be careful," he whispered, reaching out to touch a curl which hung down over her face.

"Of course I will," she hissed. "Thady's told me what to do," she added and he dropped the curl.

"Thady," he said flatly. "When can I see you again?"

"I don't know," she replied.

"It's just that the thought of you up there alone..." He shrugged. "I don't know what I'm supposed to have done, Caitriona."

"Things are quietening down," she said, pointing towards the Killbeg upland and only two spirals of smoke. "There aren't as many burnings. The Ribbonmen must be moving on."

"I hope so, but you haven't answered my question. Do you want me to begin courting you again?"

She grimaced. "Michael, if I loved someone very much – more, in fact – than I loved anyone else in the whole world, and if I had done something wrong, would I tell that someone? That is the question."

He frowned at her in complete bewilderment. "Why? Have you done something terribly wrong?"

"Would you? If you had done something?"

"Well, yes, I suppose so. What have you done?" he demanded.

"I married a man I didn't love, couldn't bring myself to love, and couldn't mourn," she replied with a little shrug. "There, I've told you. Is there anything you want to tell me?"

"Tell you? No, nothing," he replied. "Why? What's brought this on?"

"Oh, I just wondered," she said, before adding, "Michael, it would be better if you didn't visit me again."

His jaw dropped. "But I love you. Please tell me what have I done wrong?" he asked, having to shout the few last words after her as she turned and fled up the mountain path.

Michael stood rooted to the spot. That really was it? What had he done to her? He reflected for a moment. She was recovering from a great shock. Maybe that was it – she simply wasn't thinking clearly – he'd give it a few days then he would go and try and reason with her.

The next few days passed in a haze for Caitriona. On her own again. She cleaned the cottage from top to bottom, trying to erase the ransacking it had received from the constables. What she couldn't forget was Michael. He lied to her – lied to her face. Each time she thought of it, she burst into fresh tears.

Lying awake in bed she began to wonder what she would have done if he had told her. Tell him the same thing, most likely. She couldn't be with a murderer. Not again.

Michael kept himself busy, too. The turf was home and he and Liam were building their rick. He did keep a look-out for any sign of Caitriona passing by to the village but there was none. Five minutes after the rick of turf was completed, he was on his way up the mountain path to see her, Liam's protestations to leave her alone ringing in his ears but ignored. He found her sitting on the ground outside the cottage, hugging her knees and looking out across the valley. One column of smoke was rising into the sky.

"They're not gone yet," he said by way of a greeting. She jumped violently, clearly not having heard him approach. "The Ribbonmen," he added, jerking his thumb in the smoke's direction.

"No."

She began to get up but he took off his hat and sat down beside her. He would get to the bottom of this.

"I love you, Caitriona," he said simply. "I want you to marry me."

She turned to him in amazement. "Marry you?" she croaked.

"I love you. I want to be with you. I don't want you to be alone anymore. Please?"

"Michael, I..." she began helplessly.

"You love me, don't you?"

"Michael..."

"I have fifteen acres of good land and a bog. We could live up here, if you'd prefer not to live under the same roof as Liam. I'd provide for you, Caitriona, I swear it. I'd never let you be wanting for anything. What do you say?" he finished, smiling eagerly at her.

This time she did get up and walked a few yards away from him, her hands on her hips. She stood for a moment or two with her head bent before turning to face him. His heart was beating wildly.

"No, Michael," she said calmly. "I think I was meant to be Mrs Brady."

"But—" He could hardly move for shock. "I have nothing else to offer you."

"I wasn't thinking of the land, Michael."

"Then what is it? Is it me?" Climbing to his feet, he gently clasped her shoulders. "What is it about me? I'll change. I'll—"

She shook her head. "No, you won't."

"Then, what?" he asked desperately. "If you're wondering what people here will think of us, we'll move."

"No."

"Then, what is it?"

"I don't love you, Michael," she said. "I thought I did but I don't. I'm sorry, but I can't marry you."

Chapter Fourteen

Michael couldn't move or speak for a few moments.

"Is that your final word?" His voice was breaking as well as his heart.

"Yes, it is," she replied quietly.

He stared at her in disbelief. This wasn't happening to him. Liam's snoring would wake him up in a minute.

"Will you marry any of them?" He nodded down into the valley.

"No." Her tone was firm.

"But you're far too young to be alone, and far too beautiful."

"That will change soon."

"Caitriona..?"

"Could you go now, please, Michael?"

"This is madness," he cried.

"Go."

"For God's sake."

"Go," she screamed.

"Right." He pulled on his hat. "I'm going. One thing, though," he added, leaning towards her. "Have you done this before? Have you led a man on so far that he's really in love with you, then decide against him? Have you?"

She bit her bottom lip, looking anguished for the first time. "No, never," she whispered, blinking furiously.

"Then, why me?" he asked before exhaling a bitter laugh. "You must have known I'd fall for it. Well, I did. I love you, Caitriona Brady and there's nothing you can do about it."

"That's it, then?" Liam asked as Michael stormed into the cottage, slammed the door, and sat on a stool in front of the fire with his back to him. "It's definitely over?"

"It is."

Liam clenched his fists in suppressed delight. At last they were free of the damned Brady woman. "What did she say?"

"Do you really think I'm going to tell you that?" Michael snapped. He got up and went to the door. "I'm going out to get drunk."

Liam let his brother go. Michael needed to exhaust his anger and get the woman out of his system, then they could start again.

Michael went to the first sheebeen he could find, a filthy hovel with a roof of brown rotting thatch on the brink of falling in. He sat at a corner table and asked for a bottle of whiskey and a glass. The locally-distilled whiskey was very potent stuff, the best quality for miles around, and could reduce big men like Michael to muttering philosophical wrecks in no time. He poured and drank one glass of whiskey immediately before looking around the room. There were two old men he didn't recognise seated on stools in a corner near the fire smoking clay pipes full of a foul-smelling tobacco. He wasn't in the humour to join them so it looked as though he was going to get drunk alone. Then, the door opened and Malachy Donnellan wandered in, taking off his hat.

"On your own?" he asked.

"Looks like it," Michael replied shortly.

"Sure, isn't it the way? Women trouble?"

"I haven't got one anymore."

"Oh?" Malachy moved closer. "Mrs John Brady given you the old elbow, has she?"

"Yes."

"That's women for you." Malachy watched closely as he poured and drank a second whiskey instead of answering. "You won't be able to stand up if you carry on in that fashion," the older man warned.

"Don't care."

"Wouldn't give you the old..?" Malachy clicked his tongue knowingly. "She looks the type."

"You've been looking at her?" Michael demanded, grabbing the older man's coat by the lapels and shaking him viciously. "You leave her alone, she can't stand the sight of the whole feckin' lot of you."

"And you now, too," Malachy replied, managing to slip out of his grasp. "Far too used to being the champion's wife, that one."

"I know," Michael agreed miserably, returning to the table, pouring his third whiskey, and drinking it in two gulps.

"Here, let me pour you another." Malachy sat down beside him and reached for the bottle. He sloshed more into the glass before nodding his thanks to the sheebeen owner, who brought a second glass to the table, and poured himself a small helping.

"Thanks." Michael belched, feeling the alcohol beginning to take effect.

"Ah, sure, with a few more of these inside you, you'll have forgotten all about her. Isn't that right?"

"I suppose so," he replied hesitantly but picked up his glass anyway. "Slainté," he said and again drank the whiskey in two gulps.

"It's good to drown your sorrows once in a while, isn't it?" Malachy slapped Michael on the back.

"I want to – to forget her," Michael slurred. "But I can't – I love her – I've loved her since the moment I first set eyes on her at Mass."

"Another drink." Malachy poured more whiskey into Michael's glass. "You never met her husband, did you? He was dead before you came here. Killed him myself, I did," he added proudly.

Michael turned away from his glass and stared as best as his bleary eyes would allow at Malachy. "You killed John Brady?"

"I did. Such a wallop on the head I gave him with my stick. Sure, he didn't stand a chance, the fecker. He shouldn't have kept going at all, after all the beatings I gave him."

"Was Caitriona there when you killed him?"

"She was." Malachy took a dainty sip of whiskey, still on his first glass. "She saw everything."

"And didn't she try and stop the fight?"

Malachy smiled. "Ah, now, she knew better than to try and interfere, Michael."

"Well, did she do anything when he died?"

"What, cry and such like?" Malachy pursed his lips and thought for a moment. "No, nothing. When she was told that he was gone, all she did was sigh. His mother was the one doing all the crying and wailing. Herself just sighed, turned away, and led her mother-in-law home. I was expecting a right tongue-lashing but I got nothing."

Michael looked down at his fingers. Caitriona must have been telling the truth when she said that she had never loved John Brady. So why couldn't she love him?

"You ever been at a fight?" Malachy asked in a 'by the way' tone and Michael jerked his head up.

"Yes," he replied shortly. "But just to watch you all."

"No, no, I meant over in Kilmoyle."

"It's nearly died out there."

"So you've never fought yourself?"

"I must go." Michael got up from his stool, swayed and leaned against the wall.

"You have," Malachy taunted. "Haven't you?"

"You're a right interfering bastard," Michael shouted at him. "Mind your own feckin' business."

"Make me." Malachy rose from his stool.

"Right, outside." Michael pushed him out the door in front of him. "I'll teach you a lesson. I'll show you that I hate nosey interfering bastards." Michael clenched his right fist and before Malachy had time to prepare himself, Michael punched and knocked him out cold.

Liam was cooking supper when Michael staggered into the cottage. Michael seemed to be nursing his right fist and Liam turned to have a better look. The fist was red and the knuckles were beginning to swell.

"You fool," he cried. "Who did you hit?"

"Aragh, not now." Michael lowered his head into his hands.

"Yes, now," Liam bellowed. "Who?"

"Malachy Donnellan."

"Mal..?" Liam rolled his eyes. "You fool. You stupid feckin' fool. You might as well have got up and told everyone at Mass."

"Oh, shut up," Michael snapped. "I'm sick of you at me and nagging me all the time. Just leave me alone, will you?"

Liam glared at his brother. The fool. He was angry at himself for letting him go out unaccompanied.

"That damned Brady woman," he said scathingly. "It's down to her, yet again."

"Shut up."

"I wish you'd never met her."

"Well, it's over now – happy?"

Liam sighed. "I should have looked after you better."

Michael scowled then winced as he wiggled his fingers. "What? Make me join the priesthood? I'm suitable in some ways but not at all in others – a bit of a problem – that."

"What's that supposed to mean?"

"You feckin'-well know." Michael got up, went into the bedroom, and slammed the door.

Liam went to the fire and lifted the pot of potatoes off the crane. Without bothering to put on his hat, he left the cottage and headed in the direction of the village. Where the feck did Malachy Donnellan drink? Turning down a laneway to the first sheebeen he could think of, he heard the metallic clinking of a bucket and he edged slowly up the lane until he could see the disgusting shack many of his parishioners chose to get drunk in.

Peering out from behind a tree, Liam's eyes widened as he saw Malachy himself flat out cold in the mud outside the door. Pat, the sheebeen owner came around the side of the building and poured a full bucket of water over Malachy's face to bring him round. Malachy sat up coughing and spluttering and Liam expected him to lay straight into Pat with his fists, but the first thing Malachy did was to roar with laughter.

"That bastard is exactly what we need. Drunk, and he still manages to flatten me. He's fought before – I know it. We've get him, you know, Pat? We've got him. He hates the Bradys, they won't let the Brady widow go and he's angry – very angry. We've got him, Pat."

Liam rested his forehead against the rough bark of the tree. "Christ," he whispered.

Caitriona sat outside the cottage until dusk was falling. It was cold and she found herself shivering.

She had lied to Michael now – lied to his face. Of course she loved him. She had never loved anyone before in the way she loved him. The heartbroken expression on his face...tears stung her eyes and she sobbed into her hands.

When no more tears would come, she sat up straight, pulled a handkerchief from her sleeve and blew her nose. She had been lying against the rick of turf, which she'd had so much fun building with the children, before the constabulary – before everything.

She looked in on the chickens before locking them in their shed and going inside. She bolted the cottage door, then went to the bucket of water she kept for washing and cooking. Pouring some into a bowl, she gently cleaned herself. Leaving her clothes in a heap on the floor, she went into the bedroom and got into bed. She was alone and she had better get used to it because this was how it was going to be from now on. For a moment she wished John had left her pregnant, that she would have had a child by now. It was little wonder he hadn't, the number of times he had bedded her could be counted on one hand.

Michael now...turning over, she buried her face in the pillow. If only he had. If only she had allowed him to. But she had made the right decision, she couldn't help but reflect. He was a murderer. She couldn't let another murderer touch her.

When Michael woke in the morning he had a stinking headache but he forced himself to get up and eat something. He then went outside to avoid Liam's accusing eyes. The silence in the cottage was deafening. He had been drunk but he remembered everything. With one angry blow he had knocked Malachy to the ground – Malachy – the champion of the Donnellans. Michael couldn't help but smile a satisfied smile as he walked away from the cottage. The bastard had deserved it.

He was repairing a stone wall, crumbling due to wandering sheep clambering over it, when he heard his name being called. Peering along the road, he swore when he saw Malachy and the owner of the sheebeen walking out of the village. Christ, not Malachy again? Wasn't last night enough for him?

"Grand morning." Malachy gave him a grin.

Michael frowned. What was the sheebeen owner's name? Pat? He wasn't looking nearly as cheerful, which put Michael on his guard at once.

"Grand," he replied curtly. "Just passing?"

"No. I just wanted to say sorry, you know? For last night. I touched a bit of an old nerve, didn't I?"

"No."

"Ah, well, I'm sorry, anyway."

"I'm sorry for hitting you. I lost my temper."

"It's quite a temper." Malachy laughed and rubbed a huge purple bruise on his forehead.

"Yes." Michael showed him his bruised knuckles.

Malachy peered closely at them before grinning again. "You came out of it better off than me. That was a great punch."

"Like I said, I lost my temper," Michael repeated, wishing they would go. "I'm sorry."

"Aragh, forget it. But those Bradys have made you angry, haven't they?"

"Yes. I thought Caitriona loved me."

"What about the others, though?" Malachy went on. "They haven't exactly been co-operative, have they? Wouldn't change their name, even though they were asked nicely..."

"I don't think that was all their fault..."

"Yes, but it would have let you and herself be together, wouldn't it?"

"Yes." He sighed. "It would."

"Well, don't you want to get your own back?"

Michael's eyes narrowed suspiciously. "Why? What's the point now?"

"Well," Malachy began. "We need a big, strong fellow like you. I'm getting on a bit and—"

Michael noted Pat's expression of astonishment which was instantly toned down to as near to impassiveness as he could manage.

"You're asking me to join you as the champion of the Donnellans?" Michael was incredulous.

"Ah, well, not the champion just yet. I think there's a bit of life in the old dog yet."

"But you want me to join you all the same?"

"What do you say?" Malachy asked. "Teach them feckin' Bradys a lesson and put them in their place?"

"But I'm the priest's brother..."

"You're a grown man, Michael. Surely you don't need your big brother's permission?" Malachy sneered.

"No, I don't," Michael snapped and thrust out a hand. "You're on."

"You won't regret it." Malachy grinned from ear to ear and shook Michael warmly by the hand.

Chapter Fifteen

Caitriona was wringing her black dress out, about to hang it up to dry on the washing line, when she heard footsteps behind her. Thinking it might be Michael come to plead with her again, she quickly smoothed down her hair, turned and stared. It was Mary and her heart sank.

"Great morning." Mary stood with her hands on her hips to get her breath back after the climb. "Oh, that path, I must be getting old."

"How are you feeling now?" Caitriona hung the dress up and, as it was a blustery day, secured it to the line with four pegs.

"I'm fine. I just wanted to thank you for looking after the children."

"Oh." Caitriona wasn't expecting gratitude. "Well, like I said to Thady, I'm just sorry that the constabulary had to raid us. How are the children?"

"Grand now. That wasn't your fault. The constabulary are doing raids all over the place, I'm sure we'll be soon."

"I hope not."

"I hope so," Mary said firmly. "I just want the raid over and done with, the waiting is awful."

"I suppose it is." There was an awkward silence and Caitriona pointed to the cottage. "Won't you come in? I was just going to eat."

"No, I won't, thanks," Mary replied. "I also wanted to say sorry about Michael Warner. I know he was a good man."

"Yes," Caitriona lied and dried her hands on her apron. "You haven't seen anything of him, have you? We had 'words' before he left and I haven't seen him since."

"No, I haven't see him. Though, I did overhear something about a fight outside one of the sheebeens in the village last night. Michael Warner was supposed to have knocked Malachy Donnellan out cold. It serves Malachy right, the bastard."

Caitriona's heart pounded. "Michael wasn't hurt, was he?"

"Not that I heard, though, I'm sure he's well able to stand up for himself."

"Yes." She could feel Mary staring at her. Knowing Mary, she wouldn't keep whatever it was to herself for long.

"You're very pale, Caitriona, is there anything else the matter?"

"No," she lied again, before adding truthfully, "I'm just feeling sorry for myself."

"You're not..?" Mary asked, hesitantly for her.

"No," Caitriona cried. "No, I'm not expecting a baby. How dare—"

"I had to ask," Mary interrupted. "Because if you were, you'd have to go home."

"That's what you've wanted all along. Oh, feck off, Mary."

"And what? Leave you alone?" Mary took her arm and ushered her into the cottage. Sitting her down on one chair, Mary sat on the other. "You don't want to be up here on your own for the rest of your life, surely?"

"No," Caitriona admitted and tears stung her eyes.

"Then why not marry Michael Warner? He's a handsome man, a farmer, has a brother a priest..."

"I – I—" She faltered. "You just know when something isn't right."

"Yes," Mary said firmly and got to her feet. "And so do I. Come on." She reached down for Caitriona's wrist. "I'm bringing you home with me for a good feed. The state of you..." She tut-tutted.

"No, I, really—" Caitriona protested. She didn't want anyone – least of all Mary – to think she couldn't cope.

"No, I, really, nothing." Mary flung a shawl around Caitriona's shoulders and marched her out of the cottage and down the mountain path.

Passing the Warners' cottage, Caitriona's heart pounded when she saw Michael wandering through his field of corn, his hands on his hips and clearly deep in thought. In the village, they caught up with Malachy Donnellan and Pat, the sheebeen owner. The former stopped and raised his hat elaborately to them both.

"Well, now, if it isn't the two Mrs Bradys."

"Come on." Mary pulled Caitriona along the road. "Don't let's be wasting our time talking to the likes of him."

"The likes of me." Malachy roared with laughter before turning so quickly to Caitriona that she instinctively backed away and trod heavily on Mary's foot, making her yelp. "And what do you think of the likes of me, Mrs Brady?"

"I think you already know," she replied quietly. "You killed my husband."

"Oh?" He feigned surprise. "You're still thinking about him, then?"

Though emotionally exhausted, she knew he was trying in his own inimitable style to tell her something. She exchanged a glance with Mary, whose lip curled.

"Of course I think about John," she told him. "You won't let him lie."

Malachy ignored that. "What about the new man? Or, should I add, the new man that was?"

She peered at him suspiciously. What had he heard? "What about him?"

"Aha." Malachy laughed mysteriously, raised his hat to them again before he and Pat left them standing bewildered in the middle of the road.

"Bastard," Mary said loudly. "He'd confuse the devil himself, he would."

"But what did he mean?" Caitriona demanded. "He wasn't saying everything."

"He wouldn't know how." Mary pulled her along the road again. "Come on."

She wasn't embarrassed for long at the enthusiasm with which Thady and the children greeted her. Mary wouldn't let her help with the dinner and following a wink from Thady, she sat down at the kitchen table.

"Are you going to The Well of the Waters, Caitriona?" Cormac bounded across the kitchen to her. "On the Lughnasa pilgrimage?"

"What?" Blood drained out of her face and she looked aghast at Thady. "It's not that time already?"

"It's the start of August in a couple of weeks," he replied sombrely.

"Oh." She looked down into Cormac's eager face. "I don't know yet, but probably. I'll tell you as soon as I know."

Walking away from the cottage with Thady after the meal, she told him of the puzzling encounter with Malachy Donnellan.

Thady swore under his breath. "I wish that man would get what's owing to him."

"I know, but what he was saying – or what he wasn't saying – I was so confused that I don't know if I heard him correctly now," she said miserably.

"You think he's after Michael for the Donnellans?" Thady pushed his hat to the back of his head. "Christ, I wouldn't put it past the bastard."

"What can I do?" she wailed. "What if he's killed..?"

"Michael wouldn't be stupid enough to join them."

"He was very angry..."

"Even so, after all he's seen and heard in the time he's lived here..."

"I know," she whispered. "But I'm still scared."

After he had given his word to Malachy, Michael immediately began to regret it. He had been furious and Malachy had taken advantage of it, the bastard. He couldn't think of anything but the fact that he had been lured into the Donnellans by the man who had killed Caitriona's husband. He had to get out. He had to go and speak to Malachy.

Without a word to Liam, he slipped quietly out of the cottage after supper and walked quickly to Malachy's home, hopeful that he would catch Malachy at his meal. He was lucky, Malachy was just putting his hat on to go out when Michael approached the house.

"Well, sure, if it isn't the man of the moment." Michael was slapped on the back in a friendly fashion.

Michael did all he could to stop himself from shying away. He had to do this subtly, Malachy was a conniving bastard.

"Great weather, thank God." Michael smiled as they walked down the lane.

"It is. Have you all the turf saved?" Malachy asked.

"I have. The hay is next. The weather could break at any time and Liam's fancy horse refuses to eat the straw from the oats. There's no rest at all."

"Ah, sure, it's the same with myself."

"It's the hay I came to see you about," Michael began. "You know there's a pilgrimage to The Well of the Waters soon? Well, with Liam preparing for it, saying Mass at it, and the like, I'm going to be awful busy..."

Malachy stopped abruptly and turned to face him. "Out with it, Michael. You're not man enough for the Donnellans. Or is it that them Bradys are after you?"

"No." Michael was flummoxed for a moment. "No, they're not after me."

"Then what the hell is it?" Malachy's eyes narrowed. "Why have you been so set on staying out of the fights?"

"I'm the priest's brother..."

Malachy laughed. "South of here, the priests are taking part. Is it that you're afraid of what Mrs John Brady might have to say?"

"Yes, if you must know."

"You're letting yourself be dictated to by a feckin' woman. Is that it? Or is there something else?"

Michael fought to stay calm. "No, I just happen to love her."

"But she doesn't love you, Michael. Come on, she's not worth it. Or is it that you can't satisfy her? You're not man enough for her? After John Brady, she's been spoiled, is that it? Are you running away from her, too?"

This was too much for Michael to take, however untrue it was, and he hit out. This time Malachy was ready, countered the blow, and knocked Michael to the ground.

"If I had my stick I'd teach you a lesson you'd never forget..." Malachy snarled. "There's nothing so bad as wounded pride, is there? That's why I try never to lose. You've fought before, haven't you?"

"No."

"You feckin' liar. What were you up to in Kilmoyle that you had to come here and keep your nose well out of the fights? Eh?" Malachy shouted.

"Do you want me to find out? I can, you know – I'll find out what your secret is."

"You'd be wasting your time." Michael kicked out at Malachy's ankles and sent him flying. "And you can forget about me fighting for you, too." He struggled to his feet, touching his jaw.

"I'll find out, you bastard." Malachy rolled over, nursing his shoulder. "Your feckin' brother won't want to know you by the time I've finished with you."

Michael stumbled home, furious with himself for making such a mess of it. He pushed past Liam in the cottage doorway and went into the bedroom. His anger quickly gave way to fear as he sank down onto his bed. What if Malachy was true to his word and found out? He rubbed his chin as Liam came to the door, staring silently at him, and he waited for the inevitable words.

"You've been fighting."

"Never," he replied sarcastically.

"Who with?"

"Never you mind," he added then gasped as Liam grabbed his shoulders and shook him viciously.

"I do mind," Liam said. "You can't afford to get into trouble, Michael."

"I was trying to get myself out of trouble."

"Oh." Liam released him. "And did you?"

"Yes," he lied and touched his chin again.

"I'm glad." Liam sat down on the other bed.

"There you go again." Michael glared at him. "Always thinking of yourself. Christ, I should never have done it."

"Well, you did do it. You'll be judged for it when the time comes."

"Really." Michael shook his head bitterly.

Liam moved uncomfortably. "Like I said, you'll be judged for it. It's not for me to do."

"But I want you to." The onset of tears made Michael's voice low and slow. "I'm trapped. I so want to tell her but she'll never understand what I did."

"I'm sorry about that," Liam said in a flat tone.

Michael raised his head and looked at Liam through his tears in disgust. "You're feckin' not. I love her so much but I can't tell her. I just don't know what to do."

Liam got up, seemingly unable to hear anymore. "I really am sorry," he whispered. "I must go over to the chapel – confession."

Michael almost laughed as he watched Liam leave the bedroom. Confession. He had never heard anything so painfully ironic. All he wanted to do was to confess to Caitriona but that for certain would be the end – if it wasn't the end already. His chin pained him and he reached up to touch it. It had swelled and he went outside to the bucket of water. Kneeling down, he stared at his reflection in the still water.

"You feckin' idiot," he told himself. "Fool."

His reflection glared back up at him and he plunged his head down into the bucket without holding his breath. He emerged shocked at the coldness of the water and he got to his feet. Maybe drowning himself wasn't a good idea. He couldn't leave Caitriona behind. He kicked the bucket over before stamping off up the mountain path, determined to try and walk off his anger.

Chapter Sixteen

Soon Michael found himself standing shivering a little outside Caitriona's cottage. It was late and there was no light in the kitchen or bedroom. He turned to retrace his steps back down the path but the door flew open and she rushed outside armed with a poker. She stared at him in astonishment, at his wet hair and even more dishevelled appearance.

"How dare you," she shrieked. "I thought you were the constabulary coming back."

"I'm sorry for frightening you." He grimaced, somewhat bewildered. "I didn't intend to come up here."

"No?" She edged forward, frowning at him. "Have you been fighting?"

"I..." He touched his swollen chin.

"And you're all wet. Michael..?"

"I'd better go," he mumbled, turning away.

"You can't go like that." She hurried after him and he stopped. "You look a mess," she told him with a weak smile. "Come inside and let me clean you up a bit."

Like a child, he took her outstretched hand and went with her into the kitchen. He hadn't expected this at all and was a little wary of her kindness. Then again, he told himself, she probably feels sorry for you. She sat him down on a stool before lighting a rush-light and fetching a cloth and some water in a bowl. She gently took his chin in her hand, tilting it upwards, and held the cold, wet cloth to it. He winced with pain and sighed at the touch of her at the same time.

"Hold it." She brought up his hand and he held the cloth in place while she reached for a larger piece and began to dry his hair. "You have been in the wars, haven't you?"

"Christ." He got to his feet, the wet cloth falling to the floor. This was awful. She was treating him like a child and a stranger. "I'm sorry, I shouldn't have come here, and I shouldn't have come in."

"But your face..?" she protested before biting her lip. "All right, go home, then."

"But I don't want to go, that's the thing," he cried desperately. "I don't know – I just found myself here – I can't help it."

She lowered her eyes to the damp cloth in her hands. "How are you?"

"I don't want to answer that. I love you and that's it, Caitriona. How are you?"

"Oh." She shrugged before looking directly at him. "Have you seen Malachy Donnellan lately, Michael?"

His heart sank. What did she know? Had Malachy found out already and told her?

"In passing, yes," he lied.

"Keep away from him, Michael, please," she pleaded. "The man's dangerous, you have no idea..." Unfortunately Michael had, but he nodded to placate her.

"Don't let him lure you..." she whispered.

"Caitriona..." Moving forward, he bent his head to kiss her but she pushed him away.

"No, Michael, don't. Please."

"You still love me, don't you?"

"Go." She began to fold the cloth. "Please."

He pulled a face and decided to try another tactic with her. "Are you coming on the Lughnasa pilgrimage to The Well of the Waters?"

"Yes, I am. Thady and Mary have asked me."

"I'm going, too. I might see you there..?"

"I don't know..."

"Well, you never know." He smiled at her and she flushed. His heart leapt as he walked to the door.

"Michael?" she called hesitantly and he turned immediately to face her. "Stay away from Malachy, won't you?"

Seeing her imploring face, he nodded. "I'll do my best," he promised and left her.

Caitriona sank down onto the stool and buried her face in the damp cloth. She was perspiring profusely and wiped her face and the back of her neck. He had been fighting, but just to see him and then touch him...she wiped her face again. Who had he been fighting with? She stared out the cottage door at the darkening sky. Was it on Malachy's behalf? Was her warning too late? He had been hesitant to answer her.

She got up and threw out the water she had bathed his face in before clutching the cloth to her. Please don't let him become involved, she begged.

The morning of the pilgrimage was dry and sunny but Michael was nervous as he and Liam set off early for The Well of the Waters. Would Malachy force him to fight? Would he have found anything out? He hadn't been near Malachy and Malachy hadn't been near him. It seemed as though there was stalemate and Michael would have been more than happy to leave it at that if only he didn't have a niggling worry at the back of his mind as to Malachy's intentions.

A large crowd had already gathered at the holy well as they approached and his eyes immediately sought Caitriona out but she was talking animatedly to one of the Brady children and didn't see him. He stood alone on the edge of the crowd with his back to the Donnellans, waiting impatiently for Liam to finish his preparations for the Mass. Luckily, Malachy didn't come near him and he relaxed a little as he and the crowd knelt. Once the Mass was over he would leave, Caitriona or no Caitriona.

He rose as the men of each faction reached for their sticks and quickly walked away. Behind him he could hear voices and then a child's cry. Turning, he saw Thady, his wife and Caitriona bending over one of the children. The little boy, seemed to have done something to his leg and was in tears. Michael hesitated. Should he carry on and leave unnoticed or should he go back and help? He wavered for a moment then walked back and they looked up at him in surprise.

"Anything I can do?" he asked.

"Oh, Cormac's twisted his ankle." Thady picked the little boy up and sat him on his hip. "There, now," he soothed him. "I'll carry you. Thanks for asking, Michael."

"Not at all."

He stood beside them, wondering if he should leave but heard another cry, this time it was a man's and he glanced back. Malachy was wheeling in front of Tommy Gilleen and the fight would begin at any moment.

"We should go now." Taking Caitriona's arm, they all walked away.

"Shouldn't we wait for your brother?" she asked, twisting around in his grasp.

"No." Michael kept walking. "You know what Liam's like – he'll be wasting his time trying to stop them."

"Are you sure?"

"Yes, he'll be all right."

In the village, they all stopped near the chapel where Michael would be expected to leave them and walk to his cottage. He seemed reluctant to go and Caitriona was reluctant for him to let go of her arm. He was so handsome in his black Sunday coat and smelled of soap that she had relished the walk back from the well. She flushed when she caught Mary staring at them.

"Won't you come home with us for a bite of dinner, the both of you?" she asked.

Caitriona's cheeks burned. Mary knew she and Michael were no longer courting but still saw fit to invite them as a couple. Was she trying to reconcile them, she wondered sadly. It wouldn't work. It couldn't.

"Oh, I'm sure Michael's busy..." she stammered.

"No." He smiled at Mary. "Thank you, I'll come."

Thady looked grave. Caitriona met his eyes but he just rolled them helplessly. There was nothing they could do without Michael suspecting them of knowing and Mary questioning them.

"Good," Thady said. "Come on, then."

At the cottage, Caitriona wanted to help Mary prepare the meal – anything as to not to have to sit with Michael – but, infuriatingly, Mary wouldn't let her. Instead, she, Michael and Thady sat around the kitchen table, the first and last racking their brains for a topic of conversation.

"Have you started on the hay yet, Michael?" Thady finally asked.

"No, that's what Liam and I – well, me mostly – that's what I'll be up to soon. Hopefully the weather will hold."

A silence fell. An awkward silence. Caitriona knew Thady couldn't think of anything else to say and Mary was too busy cooking to contribute, pausing only to send the children outside to the river for water. Caitriona squirmed in her seat. This was awful.

"Need any help, there, Mary?" she asked desperately.

"No, I'm ready now," came the reply and Caitriona rolled her eyes.

"Father Warner wouldn't have done anything silly to try and break up the fight, would he, Michael?" Thady asked.

"No, though he's getting more and more frustrated with them." Michael sighed.

"Did you have much fighting in and around Kilmoyle?" Mary asked, placing a dish of potatoes, a smaller dish of butter, and then a jug of milk down on the table.

Caitriona's heart pounded and she fought to keep her face composed as she looked to Michael for an answer. He pulled a weary expression and nodded.

"Yes, I'm afraid so, Mrs Brady. Nothing like here, though, it was dying out."

"They knew when to stop?"

"Something like that, yes. It just wasn't as pointless."

"Did your brother get involved there? Try and stop them?"

Michael frowned and Caitriona and Thady exchanged glances.

"Liam wasn't parish priest there, Mrs Brady. The Lismoyle priest did try to stop them but – like here – he wasn't heeded, I'm afraid."

"All people who choose to fight are idiots," Mary declared angrily.

Thady cleared his throat and Caitriona peered down into her hands. Mary had obviously chosen to forget or overlook the fact that her husband had once fought.

"Yes, you're right," Michael replied and smiled at the food in front of him. "This looks delicious."

The meal passed with only mundane conversation passing between them all. Caitriona, unable to bear it any longer, was the first to rise from the table. She had to get away.

"Let me help you clear away, Mary, then I have to go."

"You will not help." Mary pretended to be angry. "You must be wanting to get home."

"Yes, I've a few things to do. Thank you for the delicious meal, Mary."

"I'll walk with you." Michael got up and she pulled a face as he reached for his hat.

"Try not to be angry," Thady whispered to her. "Mary means well. She wants to see you settled – with Michael."

She had already guessed as much. Mary simply wanted her out of the way, to be no longer dependant on herself and Thady.

"I'll walk a little of the way with you," Thady said in a louder voice but his wife called him back as he went for his hat.

"Surely you want to check on the potatoes and see how they're coming along..?"

"I…" He couldn't think of a reply and Caitriona gave him a weak smile as Michael thanked Mary and they left the cottage.

"It's a beautiful day." Michael sighed happily as they walked towards the village. Another few snatched minutes in her company. He had better savour them, he didn't know when he would see or speak to her again.

"Yes, it is."

"I think Mary was trying..." He tailed off and Caitriona glared at him.

"Then she was wasting her time, Michael."

"Well, at least she cares," he retorted and saw her grimace. Was there nothing he could say or do?

"It's no good, Michael, I'm sorry."

"Right," he said and they carried on in silence.

His heart sank when, nearing the chapel, he saw Malachy leaning back against a wall, his blackthorn stick beside him. He rose on seeing them approach and by his stiff movements, Michael guessed he hadn't fared too well at the fight.

"You feckin' coward," Malachy began. "Coward. Slinking away when you thought no-one would see you."

"Don't swear." Michael glanced anxiously at Caitriona, who was regarding them both with a frown.

"You're still a coward, Warner."

"I told you—" he shouted then lowered his voice, trying desperately to answer in such a way that Caitriona wouldn't be suspicious. "I told you that you're wasting your time."

"We agreed and shook on it, Warner."

"Shook on what?" Caitriona found her voice and Michael began to sweat.

Malachy laughed knowingly. "Do you want to tell her, or shall I?"

"You get out of my sight." Michael lunged out at Malachy, who ducked. "Go before I kill you."

Malachy took him at his word and scuttled away. Michael fanned himself with his hat and beside him, he saw Caitriona shudder.

"You agreed to join the Donnellans, didn't you?" she asked quietly.

"Caitriona..." He didn't want to answer.

"Yes or no?" Her tone was brisk and he had to.

"I did, and I immediately changed my mind but he wouldn't listen to me..."

"So you threaten to kill him? That's really helping matters."

"I'm sorry..."

"You will be, Michael," she said. "Malachy's like a leech, he won't let go. He'll suck all he can out of you first. You are such a fool and after all I've warned you – after all you've seen and heard." She shook her head bitterly. "Goodbye, Michael. Keep away from me."

Chapter Seventeen

Caitriona ran up the mountain path, only halting once to catch her breath. Michael had agreed to join the Donnellans – the Donnellans – fool! She never wanted to speak to him again. She had been right to suspect him. She had been right all along. He was violent. She had seen it in the way she had aggravated him about her getting a pistol. Then, when the constabulary came and then just now. He really looked as if he meant what he said to Malachy. She bit her bottom lip as she pushed open the door of the cottage. And Mary. She should have been more on her guard. Mary was heartily sick of her being beholden to herself and Thady.

Caitriona sank down onto the stool. In a way she couldn't blame her. Mary had had enough of a family to look after. Caitriona's gaze went to the open door and she looked out across the valley. It was time to start looking for a man she could marry.

Liam didn't know if he could put up with yet another evening of Michael glaring at him, throwing things around the kitchen and swearing under his breath. He looked at his pocket watch. Thank God, it was nearly time to go to the chapel to hear confessions.

"Off to hear everyone unburdening themselves of their evil doings?" Michael sneered as he got up to go.

"I am. Are you going to come? You haven't been for weeks."

"You really expect me to come to confess to you?" Michael cried. "You know all I've done. Actually, I was thinking of going over to Ballydrum and try the ear of the priest there. He might be a little more sympathetic, have some solutions."

"You really want everyone to know, don't you?" Liam retorted, determined not to let Michael get the better of him. "What's the use? You've done it. It's in the past."

"Is that what you tell all your confessees?"

Liam flushed angrily. "No, of course not. Michael, don't be a fool."

"Then help me, please?"

"I can't..."

"Caitriona is lost to me, Liam. You may have chosen to be alone for the rest of your life but I don't want to be. Liam..?"

"I'm sorry," Liam hurried to the door and went out.

Walking to the chapel he swore for only the second time in years. He crossed himself and anxiously looked around for fear of anyone overhearing him. In the confessional, he sat waiting for the first confessee hoping that he wouldn't have to wait long. In the semi-darkness all he could think of was Michael and how all but impossible he was to live with now.

He forced himself to turn his mind to other things and thought of those parishioners who hadn't been to confession for more than a month. Surprisingly they were those whom he would have thought would be regulars. Those involved in the fights were very regular but rarely confessed to any wrongdoing. Michael, Caitriona Brady, and Thady Brady hadn't been for almost two months. Michael could be excused for now, but the other two? Liam shrugged then heard someone enter the confessional box and it slipped from his mind.

"Bless me, Father, for I have sinned. It is a week since my last confession."

Liam rolled his eyes. Malachy Donnellan. How the man had the nerve... He listened to the usual impure thoughts rubbish Malachy spouted each week and began to absolve him, wanting eagerly to get rid of him, wondering how many Hail Mary's to give him, when Malachy continued unexpectedly.

"Father, there's something else that's been on my mind lately, something you should know about."

"Oh? Well, go on."

"It's about your brother, Father."

"Michael?" Liam's heart thumped. "What about him?"

"Well." Liam heard Malachy scratch his head. "I'm not quite sure, Father, but I think he's done something. Something he regrets. Something he wants to keep quiet..?"

Malachy ended on a high, questioning note and Liam leaned forward and glared at him through the grille.

"Like what?" he demanded.

"Oh, well..." For once Malachy was flustered, as if he hadn't expected the news to affect the priest so badly. "I'm not quite sure, but it's been on my mind for a while now and I thought you ought to know, being his brother and all..."

"Yes, well, thank you." Liam sat back, closing his eyes in relief. At least Malachy didn't know. "Is there anything else?"

"Well..." He heard Malachy scratch his head again. "It is wrong to break a promise, isn't it, Father?"

"Yes," he replied hesitantly. "Why?"

"Oh, it's just that your brother and I were having a little chat the other day and now he seems to be under the impression that it isn't wrong. Now you can tell him that it is. Can't you, Father?"

Liam didn't reply but leaned forward again and stared at Malachy in consternation as he grinned back at him through the grille.

"Is that all?" He found his voice.

"It is, Father, thank you."

Liam quickly absolved Malachy and gave him five Hail Mary's before sinking back in his seat as he heard the other man leave the confessional box. He touched his forehead and jumped, he was sweating profusely.

"Bastard," he whispered and quickly crossed himself.

He opened the door and peered out into the chapel. Thankfully it was empty and he went out and began to pace up and down the aisle. What had Michael been up to, talking to that man? What had he said to give him those ideas? Without waiting for anymore confessees, he threw open the chapel door and strode along the road to the cottage without disrobing. He stood silently in the doorway for a few minutes watching Michael, who was sitting on his bed staring into space. He went into the bedroom and closed the door to the kitchen.

Michael started up and gaped wide-eyed at him. "You're back early?"

"I had one confessee. One who was more than enough."

"Oh?"

"It was Malachy Donnellan. He told me a lot about you, Michael. What the hell have you been up to?"

Michael scowled. "Mind your own business."

"I will not." Liam ran across the room and shook him. "He suspects you, Michael."

Michael looked away. "He has no proof, Liam. The bastard's just testing me."

"But why? He was also saying that you had promised him something?"

"I changed my mind."

"About what?" Liam demanded.

"About joining the Donnellans," Michael returned. "I was angry but I changed my mind once I calmed down. He can feck off with himself now."

Liam was stunned. "You agreed to..?" He tailed off and his arms flopped down by his side in utter despair. "You feckin' idiot. You know full-well that he won't."

"I don't think I know anything 'full-well' at the moment, Liam." Michael got to his feet, clutching his head. "So leave me alone, will you?"

"Michael. Michael." Liam grabbed his shoulders, trying desperately to calm them both down. "Sit down, please. We have to decide what to do."

"Do?" Michael stared down at his brother in surprised amusement. "You know what you can do."

"Sit down," Liam ordered and Michael did as he was told. "Now." He took a deep breath. "Tell me everything."

Michael pulled a face. "He's been at me for months. Why was I not on one side or another? Why wasn't I with the Bradys because of Caitriona? Then, he suggested I was hiding something. I think he only meant it as a joke but it shocked me so much that I'm sure he saw it in my face. I couldn't help it, Liam."

"I know." He sighed. "And now he really suspects something and I think he could tell there was something from my face, too. I was that shocked. You should have told me this sooner."

"I was trying to keep things quiet."

"Does anyone else suspect anything?"

"I don't know who Malachy might have told, but—" Michael closed his eyes momentarily. "I think Caitriona might."

Liam recoiled. The damned Brady woman again. "Why?" he asked warily.

"She heard Malachy raging at me for changing my mind and I lost my temper..."

"What did you say?" he added quietly.

"That if he didn't go away, I'd kill him."

Liam sank down onto his bed. "I suppose you realise she would have to be extremely stupid not to be suspicious. And, for a woman, she isn't stupid at all. What did she say?"

"She guessed that I had agreed to join Malachy. I told her I'd changed my mind immediately, but..." He tailed off and shrugged again.

"What now?"

"She told me I was a fool and to keep away from her."

"She did?" Liam was surprised. For once he agreed with her.

"Aren't you delighted now?" Michael sneered before lowering his head into his hands.

"Next week." Liam made himself think clearly. "The pilgrimage to St Dominic's Well – you're not going – you'll be here, ill in bed."

"But I can't be ill – what about the hay?" Michael protested.

"Feck the hay," Liam cried. "If this gets out we won't need hay. We'd have to leave here."

"You'll have to do the hay, so."

"Fine. I'll do the hay. You just—" Liam sighed. "You just keep out of people's way for now."

"Won't that make them even more suspicious?"

"Have you any better solutions?" he demanded.

"No, I haven't," Michael replied meekly.

Liam left the cottage and wandered back along the road to the chapel. To his relief, no-one else had come for confession so he closed the door and knelt at the alter to think. He had noted the expression of distaste on Michael's face when he had said that he would have to be ill. Michael had the constitution of an ox and was rarely ill. He would have to do something about that.

Caitriona had a visit from Thady the following day. His eyes widened at her red eyes and obvious exhaustion and sat her down on the chair beside the fire.

"I feel terrible, too," she said, giving him a little smile.

"I'm sorry about Mary, she meant well."

"I know, but it's not her, it's Michael. He had agreed to join the Donnellans, Thady."

Thady sank down onto the stool, clearly stunned. "But how could he be so stupid?"

"He said he was angry when Malachy asked him. He's changed his mind now but Malachy won't take no for an answer. Our courtship is over, Thady," she told him sadly. "For good. That's it. I've had enough."

"Ah, lass, I'm so sorry." He squeezed her hands as she dissolved into tears.

"And do you know what else?" she sobbed. "When Malachy wouldn't go away, Michael threatened to kill him."

"No," Thady exclaimed. "Oh, Caitriona, you're right to end it. I was hoping against hope that what I was told would turn out to be wrong, but you heard him say it?"

"Yes. It's over, Thady, and—" She paused to wipe her eyes. "I'm going to start looking for another husband. At the well – there'll be people from all over there."

"Maybe it's for the best," Thady soothed. "But make sure you're sure. Don't be courted by a man just for the sake of it."

"No," she replied and added firmly, "like I said before, he'll have to be from out of the parish, I'm not going to be courted by any of the fools here."

Thady nodded. "Whatever you think best, lass."

"I'm so lonely," she admitted for the first time and another tear trickled down her cheek. "So lonely. Some days, the only time I speak is to Áine and the chickens."

"I'm sorry, lass." Thady observed her with intense pity. "If you could only come to live with us..."

"No, Thady." She patted his hands. "No, thank you. You've no room."

"I know. But don't let being lonely make you rush into anything, will you?"

"No, I won't," she replied firmly, but inside she was unsure. The prospect of going out looking specifically for a husband frightened her.

"We all have our troubles, lass," he said in a tired voice and she looked at him in alarm. "The constabulary raided us last night."

"Oh, Thady. And you still came to see me. You shouldn't have come."

"I was glad to get away. Mary's hopping mad. It was just before dawn and they tore the house apart."

"But you're all all right?"

"Ah, yes. A bit shaken, you know, but..." He tailed off and sighed.

"At least they've been now," she said in an attempt to sooth him.

"Yes." He smiled at her before getting up. "I'll see you at St Dominic's Well?"

"Yes, you will." She followed him to the door, her heart beating uncomfortably. "Goodbye, Thady. Thank you for coming."

He waved as he set off down the mountain path. She closed the door and returned to her seat. To actually have to go deliberately looking for a husband was very distasteful to her. But what else could she do? She couldn't survive on her own for much longer, she would go mad. She needed children to care for her in her old age and she needed a man to help provide them. It all seemed very cold and calculating but, she lowered her chin into her hands, what else could she do?

Chapter Eighteen

The following week, Caitriona met Thady, Mary, and the children on the road out of Doon village and walked with them to St Dominic's Well. On seeing the large crowd there, she had to make a conscious effort not to look for Michael. If she had, she wouldn't have been able to find him.

Three days previously Liam had ridden the seven miles across the mountain to the town of Ballydrum. In the dispensary he had explained to the doctor how he had been sleeping badly over the past few weeks, that because of the faction fighting, he was finding the position of parish priest in Doon far harder than he had anticipated, and that a drink wasn't helping him to sleep. Was there anything..? Ten minutes later he was on his way back across the mountain to Doon with a vial of laudanum in his pocket.

On the morning of the pilgrimage to St Dominic's Well, he woke Michael and gave him some oatmeal bread and butter followed by a mug of milk into which he had added drops of the laudanum.

To his immense relief, Michael regarded his kindness as being genuine, ate the bread and drank the milk. Within minutes he was fast asleep at the kitchen table, his head resting on his arms, and would be for hours.

Caitriona saw Father Warner arrive at the well but was prevented from looking any further by someone clearing his throat beside her.

"My friend was right." The gentleman smiled at her while taking off his hat. "You are beautiful."

She forced herself to return a smile. "Thank you, Mr..?"

"Jack Duggan." He lifted her hand and kissed it. "From Dunmorahan."

She had heard of him. He owned a hotel and public house in the town and quite well to-do. About forty-years-old, he was tall and slim but with a heavily-lined face which spoke of a hard life in reaching his present status.

"I'm very pleased to meet you, Mr Duggan. I haven't seen you here before."

"My fault entirely. If I'd have known you came on the pilgrimages to this well, I'd have been here continuously."

She smiled again. He was nothing if not a flatterer.

"May I ask you to dance, once the Mass is over?" he asked politely. "Unless you are already spoken for?"

"No, I'm not spoken for," she replied, just keeping the catch out of her voice. "Of course you may dance with me, Mr Duggan."

Thady caught her eye as they all knelt down and winked at her. She smiled weakly in reply but all she could think of was when she and Michael had first knelt down together. She tried to put it out of her mind and looked up at Father Warner's back as he began the Mass. Her eyes then began to wander over what she could see of the crowd. The priest seemed to have come alone. Where was Michael?

"May I get you a drink, Mrs Brady?" Duggan asked as they rose.

"Not just now, thank you, Mr Duggan." She took his arm. "Maybe later."

"Yes, of course."

Walking out to dance with him, she felt strangely nervous. With Michael she had been defiant. Duggan wasn't as much a stranger as Michael had been, yet she still felt uneasy.

Duggan was light and nimble on his feet and she had to make a conscious effort to keep up with him. He clearly had far more opportunities to dance than her. Soon he realised this and led her to a rock but, thankfully, not the flat one she and Michael had sat on.

"You should have told me to stop, Mrs Brady," he chided her gently as she patted her chest in an effort to get her breath back.

"Oh, I needed the practice," she gasped and laughed.

He smiled kindly at her before it faded to one of sympathy. "You must miss your husband very much?"

She looked down at her hands. "Life has to go on," she said quietly and evasively.

"I know." He nodded and took the opportunity to squeeze her hand. "Would you like that drink now?"

"Yes, please." She glanced across the field at the stall. "A small glass of whiskey?"

"With pleasure."

Once he was out of earshot, a grinning Thady ran across the grass to her. "Jack Duggan. He seems keen."

"Oh, I don't know..." She flushed.

"Jack's a fussy old so-and-so, I've been told."

"Is he?" She smiled. "I'm honoured, then."

"You are." Thady touched his hat to her. "Good luck."

"One small glass of whiskey." Duggan returned and passed it to her.

"Thank you, this is very good of you, Mr Duggan."

"Aragh, not at all." He took a sip from his own glass. "I don't get out all that often now, so I try to make the most of it when I do."

"Oh." She sipped at her whiskey, wondering what that meant. "You haven't been married?"

"No, I haven't. I've been working so hard to make a success of the old hotel that I just didn't get around to it. So it's about time I did."

She turned away and pulled a face. So he was deliberately looking for someone, too. Despite herself, she wasn't at all sure whether she liked the idea of that.

"So that's the new priest in Doon," Duggan went on. "I haven't seen much of him. What's he like?"

She turned and looked sharply at Father Warner as he walked quickly away from the well. He was definitely alone.

"Very capable," she replied. Where was Michael?

"He's young," Duggan commented. "About the same age as me, I'd say."

That made her think. She had always regarded the priest as being a lot older than her. She turned back and scrutinised Duggan. He was definitely old. Well into his forties, she could see now.

"Even so, he's a very good priest." She drank deeply and watched the priest as he disappeared from view.

Liam had seen the gentleman, someone had told him his name – Jack Duggan from Dunmorahan – make a beeline across the field to Mrs Brady. She seemed to accept his flatterings and he watched them carefully while preparing for the Mass. She smiled a couple of times, flattering Duggan in return, and Liam was almost offended on Michael's behalf. How quickly she had moved on.

He had planned to leave immediately the Mass was over but he had heard Duggan ask Mrs Brady to dance with him. She didn't seem too eager but accepted all the same. He watched them dance and crossed his fingers behind his back. If only Duggan would marry her and take her away from Doon Parish. What a relief that would be.

He was startled when he saw Malachy Donnellan wandering in and out of the crowd. He was clearly looking for someone and Liam kept his fingers crossed but Malachy approached him, taking off his hat.

"Your brother's not here, Father?"

"No, he's not. He's ill, I'm afraid. I left him in bed asleep."

"Anything serious, Father?"

"Ah, well, I don't know...I had to ride over to Ballydrum to the doctor for him."

"The doctor?" Malachy's eyebrows rose in surprise. "I hope he'll be better soon, Father."

Liam couldn't think of a suitable reply and walked away.

"Mrs Brady forgot him quickly enough, didn't she?" Malachy yelled after him. "That's women for you. You're well out of it, Father."

Liam kept walking but couldn't help agree with him. He all but ran home, eager to check on Michael and see if he was still asleep. He was, snoring a little. Liam crouched down beside the kitchen table and shook him.

"Michael? Michael, it's time to get up. You've overslept."

Despite being shaken roughly by the shoulders, Michael merely grunted and slept on. Liam frowned, he hadn't given him too much laudanum, had he? He got up. The only thing he could do was to let Michael sleep it off.

Although Caitriona had insisted it wasn't necessary for Duggan to walk her home, he came part of the way with her. She reluctantly took his arm and they walked along the road in silence until he commented on it.

"Have I done anything to offend you, Mrs Brady?"

"Oh, no." She stopped and flushed. She hadn't been thinking of him at all.

"Good." He smiled at her. "I'm glad we left before they started the fight. That Malachy Donnellan was looking furious about something."

She nodded. Malachy had probably been looking for Michael, too. She availed of the opportunity to let go of Duggan's arm.

"I'll go on alone, now. I'm taking you out of your way. Thank you for a very enjoyable day, Mr Duggan."

"Not at all, Mrs Brady. Will I be seeing you next week? It is the Mass for the Feast of the Assumption at St Mary's Well."

She stared at him. She hadn't thought about next week.

"Yes, I suppose so." She made herself smile. "Thank you again, Mr Duggan. Goodbye, now."

She hurried away, eager to reach the Warners' cottage. Once in sight of it, she calmed herself and slowed down. Passing by, she saw no sign of life at all, despite it being four o'clock in the afternoon. Anxious and reluctant, she walked on up the mountain path.

It was well into the evening before Michael stirred. He felt strangely soothed and slowly got up from the kitchen table. Once on his feet, he swayed, and had to make a grab for the wall. His head felt light, as if he were slightly drunk, but very pleasantly so. He edged his way along the wall to the door and looked out. Liam was walking towards him on his way home from the chapel.

"There you are, Michael," he called cheerfully. "I thought you weren't getting up at all today."

"Why?"

"It's the evening – supper time – you missed the pilgrimage."

"Oh." Strangely he didn't care but blinked a few times as the fresh air began to clear his head. "I wasn't asleep all day, was I?"

"You were." Liam passed him, went to the fire, and threw on three sods of turf. "Were you out drinking last night?"

Michael frowned. "No. Christ, I must have been tired. But—" He scratched his head. "I remember you giving me breakfast this morning."

"You must have fallen asleep again."

"I must have," he replied slowly. "Was Caitriona at the well?"

"She was."

"Did you speak to her?" he added eagerly as Liam brought a small hand-brush, a bowl of water, and some potatoes to the table and began to scrub them clean.

"I did not. I had enough to be doing."

A thought then struck him. "Did Malachy speak to you, then?"

"He did. He asked me where you were. I told him that you were in bed – ill."

"And?"

"He seemed to accept it."

"Good." Michael was relived.

He left the door open to let fresh air into the cottage then sat down at the table across from Liam. What had come over him today? He had never slept late before. Still, he rubbed his eyes, whatever it was, it had done him the power of good.

"Will you be seeing Jack Duggan again?" was Thady's first eager question as Caitriona invited him and Mary into the cottage two days later.

"I will. Next week."

"This is all very sudden," Mary said grumpily, clearly annoyed at being left behind. "I didn't even know you had definitely finished with Michael Warner."

Caitriona didn't want to argue with her and so replied, "I suppose it is all very sudden, Mary."

"Jack Duggan's a wealthy man. He's made a good bit from his hotel."

"I'm not concerned about his wealth, Mary."

"Then what, then?" Mary snapped. "You don't want him for his body, surely?"

Caitriona flushed, thinking of Michael's. "No, of course not. There are a lot of other considerations."

"He was kind enough to buy you a drink," Thady said helpfully."

"Yes, and he does seem to be a genuinely kind man."

"Well, don't rush into anything," Mary warned, surprising her.

"I won't."

"But you're definitely meeting him next week at St Mary's Well?" Thady gave her an encouraging smile.

"Yes, I am," she replied but she wasn't looking forward to it.

When Michael woke the next two mornings, he immediately sat up in his bed and squinted out the window at the sun. It was definitely morning. What the feck had happened to him that day? He had to make a start on the hay, no matter what Liam said. He ate a good breakfast and, armed with a scythe, headed for the field. Working swiftly, he had the field cut by midday. He had seen Liam ride back to the cottage a short time before and hoped he was boiling some potatoes for dinner. With the scythe over his shoulder, he strode across the field and went out onto the road.

Closing the gate behind him he heard the sound of feet approaching and turned. Malachy Donnellan stopped in front of him and folded his arms.

"Better, then, Michael?" he asked innocently.

"Yes, I am. I think it was some bad potatoes."

"Really?" Malachy snarled. "Well, the next time you forget your promise to me, it'll be more than a few bad spuds that's wrong with you."

Michael leaned the scythe against the wall. "I hope you're not threatening me, Malachy," he said stiffly. "I will not be fighting for you – ever."

"Well, we may just have to persuade you."

Michael opened his mouth to reply but quickly closed it again and Malachy pounced.

"What? Come on, out with it. You'd go to the constabulary?"

"I might."

"You might?" Malachy stared at him. "You either will or you won't. With our little arrangement there is no question. No-one has dared to oppose me yet and lived to tell the tale. Do I make myself clear, Michael?"

Chapter Nineteen

Michael waited for a few moments before answering, determined not to let Malachy get the better of him again.

"You're wasting your breath." Picking up the scythe, he turned on his heel and walked away.

"On your head be it, then," Malachy yelled after him. "Warn your brother that his services will soon be needed."

Michael ignored him but was uneasy as he walked home.

"Was that Malachy Donnellan shouting at you?" Liam, a fork in one hand and a cloth in the other, was standing at the fire while their dinner hung over it boiling noisily.

"Who else?"

"You should keep out of that scoundrel's way," Liam added, using the cloth to lift the lid of the pot before prodding a potato.

"How can I if he comes here?" Michael demanded.

"Well, what does he want now?"

"He wanted to know why I didn't keep my so-called promise to him."

"Did he threaten you?" Liam asked sharply.

"Yes, in a kind of a way."

"Explain."

Michael rolled his eyes. "He insinuated I wouldn't live for long if I didn't fight for him."

"He'd kill you?" Liam let the fork drop into the pot of potatoes. "My God, what a mess."

"What shall I do?"

"Well, you are not to fight for him," Liam told him firmly, putting the lid down on the table and reaching for a spoon to fish the fork out of the pot.

"Can't you talk to him? Tell him that he won't be welcome at Mass anymore?"

"I'm supposed to be encouraging Mass-going."

"But you deny them the Blessed Sacrament," Michael protested. "Malachy's threatening to kill me. Oh, I should have guessed you wouldn't care."

"All right." Liam threw his hands up into the air. "I'll talk to him this evening

As soon as he had eaten his supper, Liam walked to Malachy's cottage before he could change his mind. He knocked sharply at the door and Malachy himself answered.

"May I come in, thank you." Pushing past Malachy, he went into the cottage. The Donnellan family were just finishing their meal and stared at him in surprise. "I'm sorry to disturb you, Mrs Donnellan," he said, taking off his hat, "but I need to speak to your husband alone on a very grave matter indeed."

"Of course, Father," she replied, and ushered the children outside.

"Well, Father?" Malachy kicked the door shut after them.

"A word of warning, Malachy. You do not go about threatening to kill members of my congregation, least of all my brother."

"Come crying to you, did he, Father?"

"You harm my brother, Malachy, and I'll not only forbid you to attend Mass in Doon, I'll go to the constabulary, too."

To his consternation, Malachy simply roared with laughter. "Ah, sure, I can go to Mass over the mountain in Ballydrum easily enough. As for them fecking constables…"

"I'm warning you, Malachy."

"And I'm warning you, Father," Malachy snapped. "Mind your own business."

"Michael will not be fighting for you, Malachy, and if you harm one hair on his head…"

"Oh, get back to your chapel, Father," Malachy told him in a mock-weary tone. "You're wasting your time here."

"So are you. You've been warned."

He found Mrs Donnellan and the children huddled together just outside the door, clearly frightened at having heard raised voices.

"Is everything all right, Father?" she asked timidly.

"I hope so," he replied and left them.

Michael leapt to his feet when he entered the cottage.

"Well?"

"He all but told me where to go and laughed in my face."

"Oh." Michael sank down onto his chair again.

"You're not fighting for him, Michael," he told him resolutely. "Even if I have to protect you myself." He felt for the vial of laudanum in his pocket as he spoke.

On the morning of the Feast of the Assumption, he woke before Michael and crept about the cottage preparing their breakfast. After eating his own, he left the bread, butter and jug of milk on the table before taking the vial of laudanum out of his pocket. He added two more drops than he had done previously, stirred the milk with a knife, then went out.

Michael woke when he heard the door close, sat up and watched through the window as Liam put on his hat and walked along the road towards the chapel. The door to the kitchen had been left open and he saw the food on the table. God only knew what could happen that day, so he had better have a good feed before going to St Mary's Well.

He got dressed, tucked in, and finished both the bread and the jug of milk before going outside for some water so he could shave. Caitriona was sure to be at the well and he wanted to try and look his best. Returning to the cottage, he set the bucket down outside the front door in the sunshine then went back inside for a stool, his cut-throat razor, and a small piece of mirror. Sitting down, he swayed and leant back against the wall.

He blinked a few times, feeling very odd, but he began to shave all the same. He had to get to the well to catch a glimpse at least of Caitriona. When he began to see double, he put the mirror and razor down, and splashed his face with the cold water. What the feck was the matter with him? Whatever it was wasn't going away and within seconds he had toppled off the stool.

Approaching the well, Caitriona saw Jack Duggan standing beside Thady, Mary, and the children. Thady saw her first, waved, and beckoned her over. As she walked across the field, she noted the expression on

Duggan's face. He was gazing at her in clear admiration and when she stood beside him, he kissed her hand.

"I don't know how you do it, Mrs Brady. You look more and more beautiful each time I see you."

"Thank you, Mr Duggan." She smiled generously and smoothed her hands down the skirt of her blue linen dress. "You look very well, too."

"Thank you, Mrs Brady," he replied, taking her hand. "I think Father Warner is ready to begin the Mass."

Liam's mind wasn't on the Mass. As hard as he tried not to, he couldn't stop thinking about Michael. Had he put too much laudanum in the milk? And just look at that Mrs Brady – his lip curled as he glanced back at her – hand in hand with Jack Duggan. It was just as well Michael wasn't here to see them.

"Where the feck is he now, Father?" Malachy roared, elbowing his way through the crowd only moments after the Mass ended.

"Do not use that language to me, Donnellan," Liam snapped. "I told you Michael would not be fighting for you."

"Well." Malachy shook his stick in Liam's face. "He's asked for trouble and he's going to get it."

Caitriona danced three reels with Duggan before pleading exhaustion. Duggan took her hand and they strolled away from the crowd. She had welcomed the opportunity to be alone with Michael, but Duggan..? Her heart thumped as he walked her into the trees before stopping and turning to face her.

"Mrs Brady, since last week I haven't been able to keep my mind on anything for longer than five minutes. I keep seeing your face – your beautiful face..."

She blushed and he smiled.

"I'm embarrassing you?"

"Yes, you are," she replied. "You're an awful flatterer, Mr Duggan."

"Please call me, Jack," he whispered. "Mrs Brady, will you do me the honour of allowing me to court you? You are, by far, the most beautiful woman I have ever seen. I will be able to support you, both the hotel and the pub are doing extremely well now."

Was he asking her if he could court her or marry her? She hesitated, not sure if she wanted him to do either, but what else could she do? She needed a husband.

"Yes, you may," she replied flatly and his lined face broke into a wide grin.

"Thank you," he whispered and kissed her.

His tongue in her mouth made her want to vomit. By the taste of it, he had been chewing tobacco recently. As soon as she could, she pushed him away from her.

"Jack. Stop it."

"You'll have to get used to it now," he told her and she wasn't quite sure if he was joking or not.

"Not if you don't know when to stop," she replied angrily and he stared at her in surprise. "Now, if you don't mind, I'd like to go back to Thady and Mary."

"Oh, but listen?" he protested. "I think they're all getting ready to fight."

"Well, escort me to the road, then," she ordered. She'd had enough of him and there had been no sign of Michael.

"All right." He took her hand again and they began to walk back through the trees the way they had come.

When Michael opened his eyes he found himself lying half in and half out of the cottage. What had happened to him? The ground inside the cottage was cold and he shivered as he struggled to sit up. His head spun and he leaned back against the door frame until his vision cleared. What time was it? The sun was high in the sky so it must be midday, or near enough. Should he go to St Mary's Well? If it was midday, he would most likely have missed the Mass and Malachy would now be looking for him. Maybe he should go up there and at least try and prove to Malachy he wasn't frightened of him – that he did turn up but he would not fight for him.

That resolved, he slowly got to his feet. He felt very peculiar, just like the previous week. He shook his head to try and clear it but it was as if a dense fog had settled in his brain. He put the razor and mirror on the table, pulled on his coat, and left the cottage.

"Will I see you at the next pilgrimage?" Duggan asked Caitriona as they crossed the field.

"Yes, I suppose so," she replied absently, glancing at the crowd, divided in two as usual, with the wheeling about to begin.

"Good. May I call for you at your home? I would very much like to see where you live."

"But I live halfway up a mountain," she exclaimed.

"I'll ride up. I don't mind where you live, Mrs Brady."

"The horse will," she muttered before relenting. "Very well, you may call for me, Jack."

"Thank you...may I call you Caitriona?"

"Yes, you may." She jumped violently. It always astonished her that a man as small as Tommy Gilleen could shout so loudly. She stopped and watched for a moment as he paraded himself up and down between the two sides.

"'Couldn't get Michael Warner to fight for you, could you, you fecker?"

Her heart pounded and she inadvertently began to squeeze Duggan's hand.

"That bastard has only hours to live," Malachy retorted. "No-one disobeys me and gets away with it."

Caitriona took a quick look at Father Warner and he had paled considerably. She felt she had to speak to him so she let Duggan's hand go and, ignoring his cries for her to come back, she ran across the field to the priest.

"Where is Michael?" she demanded. "Why isn't he here?"

"Michael is at home, he's ill."

"But don't you know what Malachy could do if he finds him."

"I do, Mrs Brady." He sighed. "So, I'm going home myself now."

"But even two of you against Malachy…"

"Mrs Brady," he told her tightly. "This is no longer any of your concern, so would you go back to your man-friend over there, please."

"But, Father..?"

"Mrs Brady, please, I think you've caused more than enough trouble."

Michael was worried. What was wrong with him? He had to instruct himself to put one foot in front of the other and he could barely keep his eyes open. If this carried on he would have to borrow Liam's horse and ride over to Ballydrum to see the doctor. He met no-one walking to or from the well, so everyone must be home already or still there. He wasn't sure which he would really prefer.

Nearing the well, he began to hear shouts and screams floating down to him on the breeze. His heart sank, then it plummeted even further when he rested for a moment and pulled a handkerchief from his pocket to wipe his sweaty forehead. Caitriona, arm in arm with a stranger, was walking down the hill towards him. They both stopped and he saw her flush then pale when she peered closer at him and the state he was in. With an effort, he started off again and tried to pass them.

"Michael?" she began softly. "Don't go up there, please?"

"I have to prove to Malachy that I'm not afraid and that I won't fight for him."

"But he will kill you." Her voice dropped to a whisper and the stranger tugged at her arm.

"Come on, Caitriona, we must be on our way."

She ignored him and pleaded again and he almost relented.

"Michael..?" she wailed but it was too late. Malachy had spotted him.

Chapter Twenty

Malachy had been in the thick of the fighting but someone – Liam couldn't see who – had told him to look to his left where Michael was slowly making his way up the hill towards him. Malachy immediately held up his stick and the Donnellans fell back – as did the Bradys when Tommy Gilleen did likewise – and the two factions stared at Michael in silence.

"What the feck are you doing here?" Liam whispered fiercely as Michael knelt at his feet, his hair and face damp with sweat.

"Pray for me, Liam, I don't know what's wrong with me."

Out of the corner of his eye, Liam caught sight of Malachy beginning to edge forward and turned on him.

"Don't you dare come any closer. Would you dare harm a man at prayer?"

"I'll wait until he's finished, then, Father," Malachy replied calmly and leant on his blackthorn stick.

"This man is ill."

"Oh, he will be when I've finished with him."

"Go, home Malachy," Liam warned. "Or I won't be responsible for my actions."

"If it's all the same to you, Father, I'd rather stay here and fight your brother."

"I'm ill, Liam," Michael moaned. "Make him go away and leave me alone."

Liam rolled his eyes. There was no chance of that. What could he do? He looked out over the divided crowd, hanging on his, Michael's, and Malachy's every word. Beyond them, he could see Thady Brady, his awful wife, and their three children. Beyond them again, Mrs Brady was struggling to release herself from Jack Duggan's grasp. They seemed to be having an almighty row in the process.

"Is that the man who was courting you?" Duggan was demanding. "Is that man Michael Warner?"

"Yes."

"You still love him, don't you?" Duggan added, shaking her viciously. "I don't like to be made look a right feckin' eejit."

"Well, you know what you can do, then," she screamed back. "Kissing you was like licking the floor of a sheebeen. In fact, licking the floor of a sheebeen would have been nicer. Don't you care at all? Malachy's going to kill him," she whimpered.

Liam managed to haul Michael to his feet. Michael staggered forward and Liam needed all his strength to hold him up. He was more than relieved when he saw Thady elbowing his way through the crowd towards them.

"Excuse me?" Malachy cried innocently, grabbing Thady's arm. "Just where do you think you're going?"

"To help a sick man," Thady replied, shaking off his hand. "Someone will come for you later."

Liam smiled gratefully as Thady took one of Michael's arms, while he took the other, and they began to help him back down the hill.

"Oh, no," Malachy cried authoritatively. "I'm not finished with you yet, Michael Warner." He turned to his faction. "Come on, then," he ordered, but they remained where they stood. The Bradys were motionless, too. "Are you disobeying me?" he demanded. "You know what happens – this is what happens to men who disobey me."

He turned, raising his stick at the same time, and swung it straight into Michael's stomach. The condition Michael was in, it only made him groan. Liam and Thady kept walking – almost dragging Michael along with them – while Malachy kept on with his stick, not caring who he hit now. A blow to the side of his head rendered Michael unconscious and it seemed Liam and Thady were fighting a loosing battle in attempting to drag him away.

Caitriona kicked and punched at Duggan, eventually was free of him, and ran up the hill towards them with Duggan following her.

"Get back," Thady bellowed. "Caitriona – no."

"No, no, wait." Liam struggled to think clearly. He turned his head and managed to catch the eye of one of the Bradys who ran forward. "Take him." He off-loaded Michael's arm onto an astounded Duggan, grabbed the stick from the Brady man and rounded on Malachy. "Get Michael away from here, Mrs Brady," he yelled over his shoulder. "Bring him home."

Liam swung the stick at Malachy, who was still beating Michael, Thady, and now Duggan and Caitriona. Malachy was utterly incensed as he didn't know which man or woman to aim for now. He soon stopped beating them and turned on Liam with all his might but Liam was more than ready for him.

"Ever since I came to this parish I've had to put up with block-heads like you. You've disobeyed me. You've threatened me and my brother. You've lied to me and I'll see you in hell, Donnellan."

Even that last denunciation didn't disturb Malachy. He was clearly finding a priest of all people far harder to tackle than he had anticipated and Michael was being dragged off into the distance. Liam knew Malachy had to finish this quickly if he wasn't going to be humiliated in front of, not only his own followers, but all of the Bradys, too. Malachy lashed out time and again with his stick but Liam met and countered each blow, at last beginning to see panic in the other man's eyes.

"Come on," Liam roared, striking Malachy in the stomach and sending him flying onto his back. "Do you really want to be beaten by a priest using a Brady stick?"

Despite having grounded Malachy, Liam was far from finished with him. This had to be ended now. He beat on and on, not allowing Malachy to rise to his feet. He beat on and on until he was grabbed from behind by the owner of the stick.

"For the love of God, mercy, Father. Can't you see that he's dead?"

That brought Liam back to his senses. He stared down at Malachy's battered and bloodied head and body and dropped the stick.

"Did they all get away?" he asked, looking around at the man.

"Oh, yes, Father. Right away."

Liam nodded with relief. "Get someone to bury...this."

The man stared at him. "But, Father, that's your..?"

Liam shook his head. "Not anymore. Just bury him. Fetch another priest if you must." His hands shaking, he turned and staggered down the hill away from the well.

"Bring him to my cottage," Caitriona ordered as they left the field. Tilting Michael's head upwards, she winced and vomit rose in her throat. His swollen face was almost unrecognisable, thanks to Malachy's stick.

"Up the mountain?" Duggan gasped.

"Up the mountain," she repeated firmly. She didn't want to have to think of it, but if Michael were to die, she wanted it to be in her home. "I'll run on ahead."

In the cottage she barely took time to draw breath or examine the bruises on her hands where Malachy had beaten her. She prodded life into the fire and poured water from the bucket into the kettle and hung it up on the crane to heat before going to the stream to fetch more. Returning to the kitchen, she stood for a moment. Which bed? Hers or the one in the alcove in the wall? The hag bed was more practical, being beside the fire, but John's mother had died in it... She sighed and put that out of her mind. The hag bed it would be.

She rummaged through the blanket box in the bedroom for old pieces of cloth for bathing and bandaging and deposited everything she would need on the kitchen table. All she could do now was rest while she had the chance and wait for them to arrive.

Pushing open the door of the cottage, Liam found it empty. He stood in the middle of the kitchen floor in utter bewilderment before a thought struck him. The damned Brady woman. Surely she hadn't told Thady and Duggan to drag Michael all the way up to that Godforsaken place on the mountain? The more he thought about it, the more he realised she probably had. Wearily, he trudged outside and onto the mountain path.

It took a while for Thady and Jack to haul Michael up the mountain path to the cottage but Caitriona eventually saw them approaching and ran to help. Michael was laid on the hag bed and Duggan swore.

"Look at me. I'm feckin' ruined."

"Well, feck off, then," she raged. How could she even have considered him as a husband?

"I will." He glared at her before stomping off back down the path towards the village like a sulky child.

"Christ, look at the state of him..." Thady couldn't help but swear as they began to gently peel off Michael's clothes.

As they were doing so, she noticed the cuts and bruises on Thady's arms and face.

"Look at you, too," she whispered.

"Aragh, I'm grand. Let's get Michael cleaned up."

Michael was deeply unconscious and hadn't even stirred, despite being half-dragged-half-carried for five miles. When all his clothes were removed, Caitriona fought back tears. His beautiful body was covered in bruises, blood oozed from where the skin had been broken, and there was a large swelling on the side of his head where Malachy had struck him. Together, Caitriona and Thady cleaned and bathed him with warm water before covering him with a blanket. There was nothing they could do now but wait.

Liam thought he'd never make it up the mountain path and was extremely glad to be able to rest on a rock at a point where the path levelled off. Mopping his forehead, he saw a figure hurrying towards him. As the figure got closer, Liam recognised him as Jack Duggan.

"So she's brought Michael up here, then?" he asked.

"She has," Dugan replied shortly. "No offence to you, Father, but I think it's disgusting – leading me on like that while carrying on with your brother all the time behind my back."

Liam opened his mouth to argue he knew for a fact that she hadn't, but closed it again.

"How is my brother?" he asked instead and was alarmed to see Duggan frown.

"Unconscious, Father, and covered in cuts and bruises. Thady and Caitriona – Mrs Brady – were about to start cleaning him when I left."

"I see." Liam walked on but Duggan called after him.

"What about Malachy Donnellan?"

"Malachy has been taken care of," Liam replied over his shoulder.

He knocked at the open door and went into the cottage. Mrs Brady, kneeling on the floor, was tending to a shirt-less Thady who was seated on a stool. His chest, arms, and face were badly bruised and swollen.

"Father." She dropped a cloth into a bowl and got to her feet. "Are you all right? I can fetch some cold water from the stream for your swellings..?"

He hesitated before answering. He could not only feel a great weariness but aches and pains all over his body.

"No, thank you. I'm quite well," he lied, glancing at the bruises on her hands. He didn't want her tending to him.

"And what about Malachy?"

Liam stared at her but didn't answer. Instead, he went to the hag bed. Michael was still alive, thank God, with wet cloths draped on his forehead and cheeks to bring the swellings down.

"He's very badly cut and bruised," she said. "And that blow to his head...should we send for a doctor?"

"A doctor?" he snapped, making her jump. "A doctor won't be able to do anything. Michael's in a deep sleep, that's all. I don't want a doctor poking about at him."

"But he could die."

"I doubt if he will," Liam replied and was rewarded with a slap across the face.

"I love him," she screamed. "Even if you don't."

"I do love him," Liam retorted. "More than you'll ever know. Why do you think I killed—" He stopped.

All the blood seemed to drain from her face. "Killed who?" she whispered as Thady heaved himself up from the stool and pulled on his shirt.

Liam turned away from the bed, his mouth dry. "Malachy Donnellan," he mumbled.

"Malachy's dead?" Thady found his voice.

"Yes, and everyone saw me kill him." Liam looked around for a chair, running a hand over his swollen jaw. "I knew I couldn't be lucky twice."

Mrs Brady backed away as he sat down and she exchanged a horrified glance with Thady.

"You've murdered someone before?" she stammered.

"Yes, a constable. The constabulary were on their way to evict a family from their home and I lured one of them away – a real bastard – and killed him. No-one witnessed our fight and I thought I'd got away with it. But I hadn't quite – I'd been seen near the house – and they came looking for a Ribbonman matching my description."

She leaned back against the wall. "And they arrested Michael instead?"

Liam nodded wearily. "Eleven years ago, I still had all my hair. I looked like Michael from a distance – well, the other constables thought I did – and they came to our home the following day and arrested him."

"And he admitted to being the Ribbonman and not you?"

"Yes, he did. I begged him not to but he was seventeen and there was no talking to him. He said that he didn't want Mammy and Daddy working themselves into the ground so I could be sent to Maynooth to have been for nothing and that I, as a priest, could do more good than he ever could."

"So he was put on trial?"

"Yes. And despite having no proof that he did it, the constabulary wanted Michael to hang for the murder but thankfully the judge was a stickler for doing things by the book and sentenced Michael to ten years in gaol instead."

"You stood by while your brother went to in gaol for ten years for something he didn't do," she said, her voice shaking. "You disgust me."

"What are you going to do now?" Thady asked and Liam looked across the kitchen at him.

"Michael will be safe now Malachy's dead, but everyone saw me kill him, so I need to go – leave Doon for good. May I say goodbye to my brother in private, please, Mrs Brady?" he added, turning back to her.

She nodded and Thady followed her outside and closed the door, leaving Liam alone with Michael.

Chapter Twenty-One

Liam went to the hag bed. He picked up Michael's bruised hand and squeezed it gently.

"Mammy and Daddy told me to look after you and I didn't – I didn't look after you at all." He paused and fought back tears. "I'm so very sorry. I got rid of Malachy for you, though. He's dead, so I'm having to go. I'm going to pay for taking a life this time, I swear."

Lifting off the wet cloths, he bent down and kissed Michael's forehead.

"Be happy, Michael. Do what you've always wanted to do – read books – become a schoolmaster – teach. And make sure that damned Brady woman looks after you," he added with a weak smile. "Goodbye, Michael, and God bless you."

Outside, Caitriona's legs had given way and she had been forced to sit down on the ground. She tried to get up when Father Warner emerged from the cottage but her legs wouldn't hold her.

"Where will you go?" she asked, peering up at him and having to shade her eyes against the sun.

"I think it's best you don't know, Mrs Brady. Please look after Michael, won't you?"

"I love him. I won't let him come to any harm." She managed to struggle to her feet and Thady steadied her. "Would you like to bring some food with you? I have bread..?"

"No, thank you, Mrs Brady. I must be off at once. One thing, though." He put a hand into his coat pocket, brought out a glass vial, and handed it to her. "Laudanum. Michael may have been hit on the head but I'm sure he's merely in a deep sleep now. You need not worry, if anything, the sleep will do him good."

"I never stopped loving him," she said softly. "When I found out...I told myself that I shouldn't love a murderer...and all along he wasn't..."

"I'm sorry," he said simply and walked away.

She watched him descend the mountain path for a moment or two then peered down at the vial before exchanging a bewildered glance with Thady.

"I'll never be able to fathom any of this..." he said, shaking his head.

She turned to look at Liam Warner again but, to her surprise, he was gone. The only person she could see on the mountain path was Mary hurrying towards them and her heart sank.

"Oh, no, Thady," she moaned. "Not Mary – not now – I can't face her now."

"Don't worry." He squeezed her arm. "I'll take her straight home again. I'll be back up to see you this evening."

"Thady, no, the state you're in…"

"Hush, now. I'll be back later," he said, kissing her cheek. "Go and see to Michael."

She nodded, went back into the kitchen, and over to the hag bed. Drugged. How could Liam Warner..? She shook her head then sat on the bed beside him.

"You should have told me, Michael," she whispered, stroking his hair. "I love you. Please wake up soon," she begged but he slept on. God knows how much of the laudanum he had been given. She held up the vial, three quarters of the liquid was gone. "I love you, I want to tell you, and for you to hear me."

She kissed his lips then threw a glance outside. The sun was starting to set, so no wonder she was hungry. She sat where she was for a few minutes wondering what she could give Michael to eat? He needed to eat to regain his strength. The only suitable thing she could think of feeding him was some stirabout she had prepared the previous evening but hadn't been in the humour to eat when she got up that morning. She'd re-heat some with milk – nice and sloppy – it would slide down.

Pouring milk into a cooking pot, she added half the stirabout and hung it over the fire. She stirred the mixture until it was warm then lifted it off the crane. Pouring some into a bowl, she picked up a spoon and went and sat on the bed. Raising Michael's head, she managed to rest him back against her without spilling the stirabout.

Spooning it into him proved to be far harder than she had anticipated. The stirabout just sat in his mouth, draining out at the sides. The only solution was to spoon the stirabout into his mouth, pinch his nose, and force him to swallow. In this way, he managed to consume the entire bowl. Sitting with him in her arms, she didn't want to move but eventually hunger forced her to and she gently laid him down again. She ate the rest of the re-heated stirabout then sat beside him, stroking his face until Thady returned.

"How do you feel now?" she asked him anxiously.

"Oh, a bit stiff and a bit sore, but I'll be fine. How is Michael?"

"No change, but I did get him to eat some stirabout. A whole bowl-full."

"That's good. Well, it's true. Malachy's dead. Tommy Gilleen told me that the state of the body was shocking."

She shuddered. "I can't believe all this, Thady," she said in a small voice. "What if Michael doesn't wake up?"

"Now." Thady tried to be stern with her. "Enough of that. Of course he'll wake up – a strong man like him. We could always get Mary up here to give him a good talking-to, that should wake him up." She couldn't help but laugh. "You need to get some sleep. You know from Mammy what invalids are like, though Michael can't answer you back at the moment."

"No," she agreed, but her smile vanished almost immediately. "If he hasn't woken by tomorrow morning, I'm going to Ballydrum for the doctor, Thady. I don't care how much it costs, Michael has to wake up."

Thady nodded before walking to the bed and staring down at Michael. "Michael?" he called. "Michael, it's Thady. If you can hear me, Malachy's dead, he won't be hurting you anymore. Caitriona's here, Michael. She loves you. Be a good lad and wake up so that she can tell you herself. Come on, now." She joined Thady at the bed but there was no sign of recognition or response whatsoever. "Well, I tried." Thady sighed. "I'll come back in the morning. Is there anything I can do for him – at his home – I mean?"

"Their – his cow needs to be milked. They don't have any chickens, and Liam Warner's probably taken the horse, so that's all as far as I know."

"Right." He kissed her cheek and was gone.

Standing at the door, she squinted at the sun, sliding behind the horizon. It was time for bed. She would probably need all the sleep she could get so she could care for Michael.

She shut the chickens in their shed before going back inside and closing and bolting the cottage door. Starting to walk towards the bedroom, she stopped and looked back at Michael. If he died and she wasn't with him... To die alone must be one of the most awful things. She did go into her bedroom but only to collect her hair brush. Returning to the kitchen, she stood beside the bed.

"I don't know if you can hear me, Michael," she said softly. "But I'm going to talk to you, anyway, and tell you what I'm doing. I'm taking off my dress," she said, unbuttoning it, stepping out of it, and laying it over the chair. "And now my shift," she went on. "I've nothing on now, Michael – nothing at all. If you open your eyes you could see me naked."

She waited for a moment but nothing happened. Undaunted, she climbed onto the bed beside him.

"I'm now going to undo my hair and brush it. Do you like having your hair brushed?" Leaning forward, she removed the pins from her hair and shook it out before taking a lock and trailing it across his chest. "Can you feel that?" she whispered. "Maybe this." She leaned lower and trailed her breasts across his chest then upwards, guiding her nipples across his lips. Again there was no response and to cover her despair she pretended to be angry. "Now look here, Michael Warner. I'm not going to do all the work, you know? You have to do some work, too."

Picking up his hands, she caressed his fingers before smoothing them over her body and cupping her breasts in his palms. "Do something, please?" she pleaded. "I love you." For a moment she thought she felt his hands move and she froze. Yes, they moved! "Michael?" she whispered desperately, and his eyebrows moved up and down before his eyes opened. He stared up at her, not at first seeming to realise who she was. "It's me, Michael. It's Caitriona."

"Mmm." He nodded then winced. "Caitriona..." he mumbled and she tried not to scream with delight. "Where..?"

"You're in my home. Not in my bed, but..." She smiled mischievously and raised his hands to her lips before laying them down. "You're safe now, Malachy's dead."

He frowned. "Dead?"

"Yes," she replied simply, not wanting to tell him anymore just then. "You're safe, don't worry. I'm here and I'm going to look after you." He didn't reply and his eyes dropped to her breasts. "I thought me telling you I was naked might help you to wake up," she muttered, feeling herself blush. "It worked," she added, reaching up to cover them.

"Don't. Let me look at you," he said, and she rested her hands in her lap as his eyes drank her body in. "Oh, Caitriona, those bruises..."

"They're nothing," she replied, folding her arms and hiding her bruised hands.

"They're not nothing. They are anything but nothing."

"They'll be gone soon and so will yours."

For the first time he smiled and lifted an unsteady hand to her face. "I love you," he whispered. "I always have."

Now her tears began to flow. "I know," she wept. "I have, too."

"But that man..?"

"It was nothing, I promise. I thought you were a Ribbonman – a murderer. Now I know you're not and never have been..."

"What?" He was bewildered. "But how?"

She smiled nervously. "Your brother told me. He told Thady and I everything. Why didn't you tell me, Michael?" she asked.

"I couldn't." He closed his eyes for a moment. "Liam wouldn't let me – he wanted me to keep it a secret – so his own secrets could be kept, too."

"He put you through all that? Did he force you to go to gaol for him?"

"No," he replied at once. "No, I was seventeen and idolised Liam. I was simply very young and very foolish."

"You're still very foolish – you could have been killed today."

"I'm tough." He gave her a little smile. "I've got a hard head, thank God, the number of times I was struck by Liam when he practiced stick fighting with me..." The smile faded and he stared up at her. "Did Liam kill Malachy?" She hesitated and he pressed her. "Did he, Caitriona?"

"Yes," she whispered.

"Where is Liam now?"

"Gone. Everyone saw him kill Malachy."

Michael was silent for a moment. "You don't know where he's gone to?"

She shook her head. "He said it would be best if I didn't know. I'm sorry, Michael."

"Did he say anything else?"

"He told me to look after you. And I will, Michael," she told him. "I promise."

"I grew to hate him, you know? During those ten years in gaol, I really hated him. My parents died soon after I was arrested and they died thinking what you did – that I was a Ribbonman – and a murderer.

The authorities had no proof that I was a murderer – I would have been hung if they had – but everyone assumed I was..." Tears began to roll down his cheeks.

"Oh, Michael..." She began to kiss the tears away. "I'm so, so sorry."

"You were right, though." He took her face in his hands. "To not to have wanted anything to do with me, if I was...that."

"But I still loved you."

"I began to suspect that you knew something. How did you find out?"

"I began to suspect you – of you not telling me something. Thady found out at Dunmorahan cattle fair. I could hardly believe it, but the pistol, the constabulary – oh, Michael…"

"I don't blame you." He stroked her face. "I was – I still am very innocent. Gaol didn't help. Leaving gaol and moving to this parish didn't help either – and keeping out of the fights – I still don't know if that was a good idea or not – and then Malachy..."

"And me," she prompted softly.

"Yes. Your back, let me see it," he said, trying to turn her around.

"No, Michael." She tried to resist, knowing what he would find.

He sat up slowly and leaned over her, catching his breath and expelling it in a horrified gasp. "Oh, God, Caitriona…"

"It's all right, it doesn't hurt or itch anymore." She gasped as she felt his fingers on the scars.

"I might as well have done this to you."

"No, Michael, don't say that, please?"

"But these scars..." He bent his head and kissed them.

"They don't hurt – honestly," she whispered, arching her back as his lips moved up and down her spine.

"I'll never let anyone hurt you again," he whispered fiercely. "Least of all me."

"And I'm never letting you go, ever again." She put her arms around him and kissed his temple. "Oh." Drawing back a little from him in alarm, she reached up to touch a large lump. "Does it hurt?"

"Not anymore." He smiled. "In fact." He peered down at the multitude of cuts and bruises on his body. "You seem to have cured me, Mrs Brady." Taking her in his arms, he began to kiss her and she quickly lay down on the bed, giving him an inviting smile. He followed her down part of the way before halting and staring at her in consternation. "Caitriona, I..." He frowned. "I can't. Not now..."

"It's all right." She laid him down beside her and put her arms around him again. "We have all the time in the world now."

"So will you marry me?"

"If you're asking?"

"I am. Will you marry me?"

"I will," she replied softly. He grinned and she reached over and kissed a bruise on his cheek, one at the corner of his mouth, and finally his lips. "I love you."

"I love you. I always have. When I was told that you were Mrs Brady I was so disappointed. When I was then told you were a widow, I didn't know whether to be relieved for myself or sorry for you for your trouble."

"Someone told me you were the priest." He replied with a weak smile and she wondered if she had offended him. It was a lot to take in – that his brother was gone – and others now knew their secrets. "Sleep now," she whispered and attempted to close his eyes with her lips.

"Sleep?" He couldn't help but laugh. "All right, but before I do, I must tell you this; Eleven years ago, I had my heart set on becoming a schoolmaster. I haven't read a book in all that time, but I will do the training, and I will teach, and I will provide for you and for the children we will have. Now, come here." He drew her head down onto his chest and stroked her hair until they both fell asleep.

Chapter Twenty-Two

When Michael woke, he stared up at the underside of the thatched roof and sighed happily. Caitriona hadn't moved, she was still fast asleep, her head on his chest, her breathing slow and deep. She must have been exhausted through worry and he tried not to move a muscle to wake her. She woke with a jump all the same and he looked down and smiled as she raised her eyes to him.

"I almost forgot where I was and that you were there," she said.

"Terrible." He stroked her hair before growing both serious and embarrassed. "Caitriona, there's one last thing I have to tell you."

"Oh?" She raised herself up onto an elbow.

"As you know, I've never been married. Well—" He swallowed noisily. "How can I say this..?"

He was saved from explaining by her leaning over and kissing his forehead.

"You're a virgin?" she whispered. "You've never been with a woman?" He nodded. "Don't worry, I am, too, in a way. The number of times John and I...can be counted on one hand and even from what little I know now, he wasn't very good."

She smiled but he didn't. If John Brady wasn't very good, what on earth would he be like?

"There's only one way to find out," she whispered as if she had read his mind. "We'll help each other and do it our own way."

She began to kiss him, running her hands through his hair and all over his battered body, moving steadily lower towards his groin. It was amazing how quickly he became aroused. In seconds he was hard, responding to her gentle, teasing strokes, and he had to be inside her.

He carefully lifted his body over hers, his knees separating her legs, and she opened them wider. He slowly pushed into her, closing his eyes and sighing with pleasure as she lifted her hips to meet him, felt himself sliding into her, and gasped as she took him in completely.

Opening his eyes to look at her, he saw she was watching him, her face flushed, her mouth open as she breathed rapidly. He leaned down to kiss her then began to move.

It was incredibly exhilarating, but knowing he was giving her pleasure, and hearing her gasp each time he moved inside her, excited him all the more. His thrusts quickened, and his mouth found hers again. There was nothing gentle in his kiss now – it was passionate, demanding – and she clutched at his hips and pulled him even closer, even deeper inside her.

Her body stiffened, and inarticulate cries, gasps, and sobs tore from her throat as her fingers dug into his buttocks as she rocked against him, back arched, the top of her head pressing deep into the pillow. He felt her body tensing, and each time he moved inside her, he brought her closer to the edge, until finally, her fingers clawed his shoulders as her body convulsed.

When it was over, he held her quietly for a moment, his lips moving over her face and throat while she gasped for breath. When her breathing slowed a little, his mouth found hers and he kissed her as he began to thrust inside her again, gently at first, then harder, faster and deeper, moving toward his own release. He let himself go, surrendering to his climax with a shuddering, gasping cry.

They were both reluctant to let it end, and she held him inside her as his lips slowly moved against her throat. She turned her face to him, and their lips met in a tender kiss, which was followed by another, and another, as they held each other close. When he lifted his body to lie beside her, he felt a sense of loss as he slipped out of her. She turned to him, reaching out to touch his face as he put his arms around her.

They were just dressed and seated at the table feeding each other pieces of oatmeal bread thickly smeared with butter for breakfast when Thady arrived. He cried out in delight and shook Michael's hand with gusto.

"How do you feel now?"

"Grand," he replied with a grin, and Caitriona squeezed his knee under the table. "Thank you for doing what you did yesterday, Caitriona's just told me."

"Aragh, now." Thady dismissed it with a wave of his hand before glancing at her.

"Michael knows everything," she confirmed and Thady turned to him.

"I'm sorry, Michael, but there's no sign of your brother at all. I called to the chapel and found a letter nailed to the door." Pulling it out of his coat pocket, he passed it to Michael. "Mary read it for me – your brother said that you were innocent of all the crimes you were in gaol for, that he was the criminal, that he won't be back, and that he will write a letter of resignation to the bishop – we'll have a replacement priest soon."

Michael nodded. "And Malachy's dead."

"Yes, and buried now, too. We've seen the last of him and his like. The fighting is over in this parish. With John and now Malachy dead, Tommy Gilleen has disbanded the Bradys and the Donnellans aren't putting forward a new champion."

"Liam did do some good, then." Michael reached for her hand and kissed it. "Well, when this new priest arrives, one of his first jobs will be to marry us."

Thady's face broke into a grin and he hugged them both. "Ah, that's great news, that is surely."

"Mary will be pleased," Caitriona added and Thady roared with laughter.

"Just wait until I tell her – the face on her…"

"Look." They walked to the door and Michael pointed across the valley. For the first time in weeks, there were no burning houses and rising columns of smoke on the Killbeg upland. "Hopefully, that's the end of the Ribbonmen in this area."

"I hope so." Caitriona slipped an arm around his waist. "Even if it isn't, at least the faction fights are over in this parish so we can deal with whatever the future holds."

She met first Michael's eyes then Thady's. Both men nodded in agreement.

THE END